■ □ ■ □ ■

THE SILK, THE SHEARS
and
MARINA; OR,
ABOUT BIOGRAPHY

Writings from an Unbound Europe

■ □ ■ □ ■

IRENA VRKLJAN

THE SILK, THE SHEARS and MARINA; OR, ABOUT BIOGRAPHY

Translated from the Croatian

by Sibelan Forrester and Celia Hawkesworth

NORTHWESTERN UNIVERSITY PRESS

EVANSTON, ILLINOIS

Northwestern University Press
Evanston, Illinois 60208-4210

Printed in the United States of America

ISBN 0-8101-1603-0 (cloth)
ISBN 0-8101-1604-9 (paper)

Library of Congress Cataloging-in-Publication Data

Vrkljan, Irena, 1930–
     [O biografiji. English]
     The silk, the shears; and Marina; or, About Biography / Irena Vrkljan ;
translated from the Croatian by Sibelan Forrester and Celia Hawkesworth.
        p.   cm. — (Writings from an unbound Europe)
     ISBN 0-8101-1603-0 (cloth). — ISBN 0-8101-1604-9 (pbk.)
     1. Vrkljan, Irena, 1930– . 2. Authors, Croatian—20th century—
Biography. 3. Tsvetaeva, Marina, 1892–1941. 4. Poets, Russian—20th
century—Biography. I. Forrester, Sibelan E. S. (Sibelan Elizabeth S.)
II. Hawkesworth, Celia, 1942– . III. Title. IV. Title: The silk, the shears;
and Marina. V. Title: About biography. VI. Series.
PG1619.32.R53Z4713   1999
891.8'285409—dc21
     [B] 98-46976   98-46976
                                                                            CIP

The paper used in this publication meets the minimum requirements of the
American National Standard for Information Sciences—Permanence of Paper
for Printed Library Materials, ANSI Z39.48-1984.

■ □ ■ □ ■

CONTENTS

■ □ ■ □ ■

THE SILK, THE SHEARS

Translated by Sibelan Forrester

My mother sits in a room on the fourth floor in Zagreb and cannot express her anxiety. My sisters live in their kitchens far away from each other. Around them children shout, soup boils on the stoves. In Homburg, on Palmotić Street. The partisan V. is dead, the Bosnian mountains are left behind. My father lies in Mirogoj Cemetery, section nineteen, grave number four. One painter, a friend from the provinces, didn't find his redemption.

Thirteen years of living in West Berlin. My friends in Charlottenburg, in Steglitz. Claudio encouraged me, Benno made space on his desk.

Virginia Woolf. Charlotte Salomon. Women who wish to flee from childhood. The call of false submissiveness. For anger. And for recollection.

■ □ ■ □ ■

I
CHILDHOOD IN THE KINGDOM

The Wire

"The Gypsy is here, let her in!" I sometimes cry out in my sleep. It's the same person who, if she survived the concentration camp in the war, once again sells roasted corn on the street in front of Saint Sophia's Orthodox Church. The church was at the end of Saint Sava Street in Belgrade, the capital city of the Kingdom of Serbs, Croats, and Slovenes, where I was born. The sons of the land were traveling then, looking for work, through the former Austro-Hungarian monarchy, and so at the end of 1920 my father came to Belgrade by way of Varna and Graz and found employment as an agent for the Weinschenker Corporation. My mother, born in Bosnia, came from Vienna and found work as a secretary at the Belgrade office of Siemens. They married, and later moved with me onto that street. It was broad and white, the houses new, it smelled eternally of roasted corn. Gypsies squatted on the pavement. Their small, rough hands turned the cobs over the fire and were completely black. "You're not supposed to eat that corn from the Gypsies," my parents would say. Much later, when I came again to Saint Sava Street, it was narrow, gray, its houses dilapidated. I ate corn in front of the church with pleasure.

In the yard of the house, in the royal city of that time, low barbed wire wound around two patches of trampled grass.

Once while playing I fell on that wire, blood ran, the janitor bandaged the wound, they took me to the hospital. At that my mother, in some other, Catholic church, vowed that she would never intentionally terminate a pregnancy if I remained alive.

Above that yard was a balcony where stern-looking Father would stand in the afternoon. I played "doctor" in the basement with Gordana, the janitor's black-haired daughter. Once we stripped naked, we investigated each other above the thighs with a safety pin. Something forgotten, horrible? I wasn't allowed out into the yard anymore. "Gordana is a bad girl, a bad girl!" my parents shouted. The impossibility of escape, desolation. From then on I had to play with Lotte, the daughter of Mama's friend. They had a small house of their own, they loved power and thought that they were better than everyone else. Because of that you had to speak German with them, even at home. I still didn't know that it wasn't the local language and so I grew up bilingual. Gordana and Lotte. Downstairs and upstairs. The joints of the old dolls' limbs have been rusting ever since. I still see the blood on the barbed wire, I still smell it. But the flagstones of that yard, bordered with tar, have disappeared. Only the wire flies everywhere, lies all around. Barbed wire—*Stacheldraht*. The blood between two languages.

Besides the yard there were also foreign places. We would spend the summer vacation in Begunj, in Slovenia. There my mother's mother, a certain von Rukavina, would come to visit from Vienna. When we went for walks she tied a thin chain to my hand so I wouldn't run away. Under the great chestnuts of the hotel, Father would play chess with the village priest. Disgust at lunchtime because of the chicken skin. Swallowing, secretly drinking water. Nausea. You have to clean your plate. Always the last one at the table. Father and that priest have been moving the black and white figures for

a long time now. So under the shadowy trees of various summer vacation spots unfolds the torture of a good upbringing,
senseless punishments firm the torso of a society that insures
itself against ruin with such rituals. It sees its most important
goal in a clean plate, and to this day spends its vacation in
haughtiness, in days without luster. So too they banned the
little, sour Slovene apples. I wasn't allowed to eat them, in
the name of those new ones, beautiful and poisonous, the
kind you see today. Green apples, which fell into the grass
almost soundlessly, together with the bees. Today one of the
hotel owner's sons whom I played with then sells the old
songs of his land, adapted and unrecognizable, to television
stations in Germany. He has forgotten everything: the old
songs and the little apples.

The low room in Vinkovci was also a foreign place. Hard
clay paths to the doors of the house, the sun shone and
burned on them. We were visiting Mama's friend. The two
of them sat in the garden, drank cold juices and chatted for
days on end. The friend, very tall and very blond, was an
angel, but a snappish angel among darkly dressed and stoop-
ing peasants. Her son and her daughter caught butterflies by
twilight and stuck them on slender pins. They kept the
boxes with glass lids in that low room. I wanted to catch a
butterfly too, but it flapped wildly in my hand and I let it go
right away. A fine, brown dust remained on my fingers. The
children laughed at me spitefully, saying, "It was stupid to let
it go, such a wonderful specimen, and when you touch a
butterfly and wipe the dust off its wings it can't live any
longer anyway. Look for it, look for it, it must be lying
somewhere dead in the grass." I desperately begged my
mother, who was sitting in a white lawn chair, to take me
home. The angel's children laughed, Mother laughed too.
People who think they know best always teach us something
bad. And I realized that stopping halfway means the same
thing as going all the way. We have to beware of beginning.

Ever since, the fine brown dust always reminds me of the pin that follows after it.

Crosses

Death. It sounded for the first time in the sublet room where Papa's widowed mother lived. Grandma had a big jewelry box of black leather that I was allowed to play with. In it she kept yellowed letters, a dry corsage of violets, a brooch with a false stone, Austro-Hungarian medals, bunches of music paper, her own compositions, waltzes she played around 1900 in a tavern in Ruse in Bulgaria. Grandfather sat next to her, protected her from the drunks, and turned the pages. He had abandoned her at the beginning of their marriage and after many years she found him there, sick and in the grip of alcohol. And so she played in taverns and fed the family with her knowledge from music school in Zagreb. Her husband beat the children terribly, there were six of them. They all just died off like flies. Only my father remained, burdened until his death with hatred for his parents. There was a letter in the box from his ten-year-old brother Sasha. That scribbled letter, the black box, Grandma's stories about the spice trade of her childhood, ice-skating and playing, her departure from Yugoslavia, the catastrophes of dying. Little Sasha who died of a common cold, Vladimir who died at four probably from an inflammation of the brain, the little girl who was mowed down by typhus. About those little ones who died right after birth, Boda whom she left with strangers when she set off to look for her husband, who took his pillow and stayed out in the woods for three days, who fell into a barrel of rainwater and almost drowned, who was bit in the face by a dog, who once almost burned up. All those stories, and photographs of a stately woman in a big hat taken somewhere in Varna when they had money again for two years and Grandfather wasn't drinking, all that just settled into me, colored the beginning, it was like the grounds of some long-drunk coffee. That grandmother, whom I later visited in the asylum, wore a ribbon of black velvet around her neck. Scents from old cupboards reigned in her room, she recalled her graves without consequences. She didn't see any connection in it, she talked about everything as if she were talking about a storm or bad weather. She didn't know that people can defend themselves, and so she died in a madness which was also gentle and small. They buried her in the autumn in the asylum hospital cemetery, and Father went to the movies that afternoon after the burial. My mother reproached him for that. The black box disappeared in a move—her music, all the letters, that life.

My mother's mother died many years later in Vienna. My aunt had them pierce her heart with a pin so that she wouldn't wake up in the coffin. She got a marble cross, the other grandmother a wooden one. It was visible from the train until they redug the grave. But even today the tree-lined road that leads to the Vrapče Asylum smells of death, of the dress my mother was wearing, of dark afternoons sitting in her lap, of a room with a big icy mirror, and of the child in it. Of Father's name, Bogdan, Mother's name, Mary, Grandpa Djuro, Aunt Helena, who sometimes arrived from Vienna, wrapped in the sharp scent of eau de cologne 4711. Lorgnons, big hats, fur coats. Decay and ruin. In 1934 they took me to a hall where a black carriage stood. On a white bier an empty, golden uniform. A high, stiff collar with a hole in it. Spots of blood. The king has been killed. Many people in the hall are crying. The hole and the collar must not be touched. Some people say, the new King Petar is young and handsome, long live the monarchy! People talk about fine dresses, big hats. And they think there are no moths living in the red plush of the throne.

Before starting school I would leaf through Papa's books. Many of the bindings were done during the Secession, they always seemed a little forbidding. Albums with postcards, Italian madonnas, Murillo's boys, photographs of the mines where Father sold drilling machines. Pictures from Vienna, Mother's brother in uniform, the one who drowned at eighteen on an Easter boating trip because he was wearing heavy officer's boots. Grandmother knelt on the shore and called for help. They never found him. Bright-colored cards, Bellini's squarish bodies, blood from the breast, Morgenstern's poems beneath the gallows, Böcklin's *Island of the Dead,* Raphael, Adriaen van der Werff, Heine's poems. "The mother stood at the window, the son lay in the bed." Late afternoons, pale curtains, mysterious pictures, and the text: "On his death-bed, in bed lay the son."

Golden threads in the gray ribbon of days—those are the birthdays, name days, Christmas. Holy days in the three rooms of the apartment, always indoors, never on the street, never with others. Money, success, and gift giving are celebrated in hiding, on the premises. The more presents there are, the better we're doing. For we are somewhat better than the rest of the world, Papa and Mama love each other on those days. They don't fight. At that time I loved Ana, the servant in full skirts. She was from the Banat, she had a boyfriend and got fired because she was always kissing me, and she wasn't especially clean. They even wanted her to give up the boyfriend, whom she stood embracing in the kitchen every Sunday. She retaliated wonderfully with a yell, packed her trunks, in spite of their protests pressed one more kiss on my forehead, and disappeared. Her skirts from the Banat rustled proudly as she departed, and her white skin remained in a child's memory without a single blemish.

The details of those days have melted into one: bed, room, dining-room table. Sundays, the empty ones, change in memory. Father was suddenly earning more. A new apartment, different, business friends would drop by. They pulled a Sunday dress on me and we went visiting down steep streets, down the cobblestone pavement. Once a month to a white villa with a garden. There I would play with Miki, the dreamy son of a small businessman. Today he is half-blind, a professor in Belgrade. They lived in their own house, and the attic was finished as a playroom. An upside-down table with blankets turned into a boat, with islands around it, the sea. In the attic there was a puppet theater too, a king, a queen, it couldn't have been otherwise. The mamas would interrupt these journeys with loud calls. They were afraid of the silence in the attic, we knew that. All the same, in that world of ours there wasn't a single shadow of forbidden play, and I never had anything to say when my friends would tell stories like that from childhood. What could there be? Miki went to the French school, he wore, oddly enough, a French beret, and we traveled to our islands. Miki never escaped from the closed world of that house. Not even when the house got old and became impractical. He stayed in it, a prisoner of fidelity to possession, in its basement he almost lost his head in the war. He almost goes hungry because of the constant repairs, he sits half-blind by the window of his old nursery, and he'll die in that deserted ruin with Greek words on his lips.

They soon packed me off to the German-Serbian primary school. Mrs. Bugarski was overshadowed by the handsome German teacher Schuetz, who later died on the eastern front. We didn't like her classes. Almost all the children were from middle-class families. Zoran later wound up in prison for smuggling American cigarettes, Mihajlo became an airplane designer and emigrated to Switzerland in 1947, infatuated with jazz. Damjana—her father was a well-known doctor—found a rich husband. Jelka—her father was an adjutant to the queen—talked about life at court. Today she lives in Ljubljana, her brother recently died in an accident in the mountains. Mirjana played tennis, Ivan V. became a poet. The devotion I felt to them has disappeared just as their faces have in recollection. Father was losing himself more and more then in the world of Boehler Steel, his work was visible in new furniture, in new beige-colored china with red tulips, in new blue cups, very thin, in the expert cook, a pink ostrich-feather jacket for Mama and a big picture by the Viennese painter Neuboeck. Piles of linen and bedding grew in the cupboards, new dishes in the china cabinet. And what else, what was all that? My parents would go out in the evening to the Majestic or To the Russian Tsar, guests arrived and departed, they danced the tango. I unaccountably refused to say "I kiss your hands," I didn't want to go obediently to my room and disappear obediently into bed. Exasperated fury on all sides. On the threshold between the nursery and the room with the guests drinking sparkling wine, Father's heavy hand once and for all taught me passivity in the face of violence. I no longer believed in justice. Ties with others grew thin, and since then every act of violence by someone stronger brings nausea. There was a stink of alcohol, Father's laugh abruptly turned into a roar. I hated those festivities, the fine china, the guests. A lot of light, that means pain, so it seemed to me, and I ran into the small dark bedroom. I hid myself there.

The Pattern

Between the department stores and the empty evening streets of Wilmersdorf, where the young people in exotic garb believe that they have finally freed themselves from the dazzling advertisement of the West, that little shop in Belgrade from long ago always appears to me. The shining silk in bales, its beauty, the soft velvet, the smooth wood of the counters, Mother's hand passing over the satin, the dazzling colors. Turkish coffee in the back room, dust on the street outside, the deathbed odor of the cotton. That picture from long ago then goes quickly and fearfully back into the depths, looks for warmth and shelter, changes color, but never ages. The seahorse pattern on the silk slowly unfolds on the sales counter and remains in recollection at that movement. The creases of the silk are eternal. The shears that cut had ornamented handles and were dull. The scratches of the shears on the counter have outlived everything: the purchased silk, its pattern, my fear. Because they hurt the little horse, they cut it in half. Its head stayed behind in the shop, in the bale of silk on the shelf. Its body rested for a long time in the hem of that worn-out skirt.

A girl's upbringing. Sometimes submission with pleasure. I accompanied mother to Mr. Doroslovac's cosmetic salon, I was fascinated with the rejuvenating perfumes. I accompanied her to the hairdresser's and found that dyed curls were beautiful. Chosen as a housewife's companion, I looked into the same shop windows. In spite of that, and in fact illogically, I chose my neurotic father more and more often. He signified that other, meaningful life outside—knowledge, books, conversations. When he wasn't in the house, time passed in the everyday dusting, in purchases, washing clothes. But I didn't pass Mother's light blows on to dolls, I didn't like to play with them, I didn't feed them. I hated the imitation of maternity, I didn't learn to cook for them. But I am still nothing more than an exact reflection of the capabilities that my mother possessed, or did not possess. She didn't cook much either, I am her imprint, a copy, her miniature. I tried to cross to the other shore to the deceptive self-sufficiency of the male world, I didn't perceive the interchangeability of roles, I quickly ran aground on unfertile shores, coquettish and a little dull in my gestures. Attempts to escape looked futile. Relapses. It left a gloomy masquerade in front of the mirror, a dance with hat and cane, once again silk, ornaments, and trifles. The imprint of a little woman, a doll's doll. All the rooms turn into structures of rubber, silk ringlets, and glass eyes. And so I began to break the dolls' arms and legs, and to get only books for my birthday.

Hatred, interpreted as a love for reading. It got to be that, but by a detour, through bad children's books and comics. I dug my fingernails into my palms, no, we aren't dolls, I feel that. I cut off my long curls on the eve of March 27, 1941.

We were standing at the window and looking down into the street. There a multitude of people moved in waves. "Better war than the pact!" I couldn't find out from anyone who those people were and why they were shouting. My parents closed the window and we went to bed. That and the birth of twin sisters were the prelude to the war. Sunday April 6 brought curtains of glass dust and an incomprehensible scorching heat. The wailing of bombers, detonations. Rudely dragged out of bed, weeping in the basement where people sat on the coal, fire, later a bloody hand on the electric wire, fragments, rubble. I understood nothing of all that. Nothing of the escape from Belgrade in a train full of women and children. A rain of bullets fell suddenly, we could see the German pilot, he was flying so low. We lay along the tracks, the wood of the wagons no longer offered any protection. After the attack people got up again, but not all of them. The dead remained lying in the grass and we continued our journey. In front, on the locomotive, a white sheet from our trunk fluttered quite in vain. In the evening we came to Zagreb. With two pieces of luggage. Everything stayed behind, the blue cups and the fine china were lost. When Father went to Belgrade for the things there were already Germans in the apartment. But he found the furniture. He surely spoke German. All the rest was chalked up to fate. We fled to our relatives in Zagreb, where a quisling government had proclaimed the Independent State of Croatia. And everything began from the beginning: work, salary, Boehler Steel. People believed: Everything will be fine, the war will only last a few weeks, it's nothing, nothing terrible, only a small misfortune of history.

I still had a fear of noises. If a door slammed somewhere, I would throw myself onto the floor. They called the doctor. He consoled the family with time, which heals everything. Even regret for the attic with the islands, for the seahorse on the silk.

Aunt Viktorija's apartment, where we lived at first, was an old-fashioned three-room apartment with dirty windows. In the long, dark corridor stood cupboards, jars of cherries-in-rum in them, and it always smelled of food. The little armchairs in the room were red, the dog Jacky always lay in one of them. When I stroked him my palm was covered with a layer of brown grease. It would rub off in black crumbs. The spoons gave every soup the sourish taste of metal. The lamp burned above the table even in the daytime. My aunt's sons were interested only in acquiring provisions, they bought flour and sugar by the sack, and so the sacks stood in the corridor too. But there was also a yard with a big tree in it. I would sit under it for hours and stare at nothing. That tree and my great-aunt's indestructible flowered dress that smelled of mothballs and shortening, that was all that remained in me. No knowledge of the war, the Germans, the partisans in the mountains. Those were empty days in the old aunts' house. Viktorija had two more sisters, they lived on the ground floor, all the three did was cook, play solitaire, and cook. My forgetting Vinogradska Street expresses resistance toward them. It still reminds me of their old, wrinkled skin, dull boredom, and the stink of rats spreads in its basements.

The rest of the 1941 school year, in a parochial elementary school, has also gone into oblivion. After that we lived two months in a building on the former Ban Jelačić Square. The Central Apothecary is in it now. All that's left is the recollection of glass doors with a patch of sun on them. Then we moved to a building at 10 Buconjić Street. A bedroom, a dining room, Papa's office, the nursery, and the room between all of them, in the middle of the apartment, where I slept. I was in everyone's way then, I didn't have a table for studying, and I would take refuge again in the girls' room, read there. The family was occupied with my sisters, and soon a cook came. And guests, dancing, dinners. I collected pictures of actresses, Marike Röck, de Kowa. I hated movies about Popeye and the spinach that strengthened his muscles. I cried because of little Shirley Temple's broken glass ball, because of stupid songs on the radio—"Buy Me a Colored Balloon"—that I liked to listen to. A smooth, unenlightened middle-class world. So much sweetness leaves traces.

At age eleven they sent me to high school to be taught by the nuns. White kneesocks, black smocks, pigtails. I fell in love with young Sister Estera, she taught biology, and so the young schoolgirl also wanted to become a nun. Estera loved her protégées with the love that is born in lonely empty dormitories, and she showed us her closely cropped hair under the white cap and her flattened, wrapped breasts. She later left the convent, got married, and for a long time kept on writing to me. In the photograph she enclosed she was fat and had no aura, the man beside her was bald.

Then came Good Friday. Beneath the organ lay a painted wooden statue of Jesus and people threw coins onto it, gifts to the church. I didn't want to go to mass anymore. Somewhere in that church of Saint Blaise, which looked like a Turkish steam bath, between the pictures of saints, between the uniforms and the smugglers, somewhere in that chaos of ignorance and instinct—one old woman kneeling in Zrinjevac Square with a yellow star on her coat had to clean the high boots of some German officer—somewhere in some corner of family life, I stopped drawing queens, beautiful ladies, Mama's ball gown. A small jolt of feeling passed through the colors and daydreaming, and it tore, crumpled, all the fairies. The remnants of those drawings later yellowed in my mother's drawer. Finished, the end. With my pencil I drew trees, cypresses, I blackened pieces of paper from edge to edge.

The year 1941: First I wanted to become a nun, then on Sundays I no longer wanted to go to mass, the first books by Šenoa, Gjalski. In class we had to greet the teacher with our hands outstretched, we had to join the Ustaše supporters. I no longer drew pretty dresses, I was in everyone's way.

The owners of the house in Buconjić Street, the old Šlezinger couple, lived on the ground floor. Above us lived a colonel who was driven home by a soldier in a car. His sons were on the eastern front. I didn't know that the Šlezinger family had been driven out of that apartment. I also never heard that they were Jews. One day there was a soldier standing in front of their door on the ground floor. At the window, in the garden behind the house, Mrs. Šlezinger told me softly that they weren't allowed to leave their apartment. In the evening I climbed down from our kitchen balcony into the garden so no one would notice and gave her a bar of chocolate through the window. The next day their apartment was empty. Someone in the house said they had moved. I learned about the night transport, by truck, only after the war, from their grandson Darko Suvin. The Blau family, acquaintances of my parents, committed suicide. That too I found out only in 1945. Papa's friend, the painter Sirovy, killed himself also, somewhat later. Arrest warrants on the fences. Zarah Leander sang on the radio. The occupation. "Lili Marlene." German soldiers in the city. The central post office was blown up. Later I got to know the husband of the clerk who belonged to the illegal group in the post office and who carried out the diversion. Jasenovac concentration camp, corpses floating down the Sava. The Jews who had suddenly disappeared, who were sent away, killed. Why did no one tell me anything? "Not in front of the child," Papa would say sometimes, as I came into the room. Death in the land, German films in the movie theaters. That horrible mixture. Air attacks, a child of eleven, senseless upbringing, you must clean your plate, I kiss your hands, to bed at eight.

I see that child in a gray, empty street. There is no one beside her. Today at family funerals I don't wear black. A changed feeling, but it is still a feeling along with a costume, without color. Amazed, humble, and full of anger.

Bad Deeds

In the nuns' high school we cut little shirts out of the graph paper from our arithmetic notebooks. For each good deed we drew a cross in one square with a pencil. When the little shirt was full we would hand it in to our homeroom teacher Sister Agnes. Then she would give us a holy picture for a prayer book and with gentle handwriting would jot down some pious wish for our souls. Agnes was very pale, quiet, had tuberculosis, and was a saint to us. I visited her once after the war in the convent on Frankopanska Street, when the nuns' high school no longer existed. She was still pale, but the charm of dependence had vanished. Outside the school hierarchy she was only pretty, and we could no longer have a conversation about anything. She was uncertain without the school chalkboard behind her back, and I could no longer look at her with an agitated heart, and so I quickly left Frankopanska Street and never visited her again. I no longer know what good deeds it was we drew little crosses for on the little shirts. But I know very well what I considered bad deeds then. And when I stole some sugar once in the larder, I had the feeling, because of the little shirt, that God's three-cornered eye saw everything through the ceiling, that it was examining me through the clouds, and I ran in fear from the cool room. Afterward that eye followed me through life for a long time, Anges's stories about going astray were firm inside me. I also had a troubled conscience for wishing that Sister Estera was my mother. At night I dreamed that she lived with us and that I was allowed to hug her. I hoped that she could protect me differently from Mama. Along with these swelled the awful dreams, the ones from movies. The movies were a place of great escape, a refuge. Films were important so that at night I could play all the roles of all those beauties I had seen, so I could dance, love with their faces but with my feelings, and be embraced by Gustav Fröhlich or Viktor Stahl. I sinned every night, pulling the empty and adult face of Marike Röck or Kristine Söderbaum onto a child's body: And I believed these faces were connected with happiness, love, life in a cabin in the snowy mountains. The evil of hit songs, steps in unison up the illuminated stairs, the evil of furs, pearls, and kisses lasted a long time. Compared with my own life, they became the painted scenery of my main goal: those biographies, which were not real ones, those made-up lips. I was already grown up when I finally freed myself from the chains of the movies. Once I began to feel nauseous watching those old films I could save almost nothing from that world. I was as suspicious as a teetotaler who is offered alcohol. But when we finally deny ourselves those kinds of dreams, then at night there is no more music and dancing. The beds we lie in are strangely narrow and cold after the ones built of foam and glitter. Then came the wish for a storm or some fire to destroy all the spinach fields, for the pans of spinach or chicken in the kitchen to fall on the floor, for everything they held to pour out, empty out, and for my plate on the table to remain empty. Or full of my favorite macaroni. I often wished that Papa would leave on a business trip, that Mama would stay forever with her friends in the café, so I could be alone for a long time in the house, could eat as much chocolate as I wanted, and could dream in peace. I went to swim in the Sava with a bad conscience, because I was happy to get away from all of them. I didn't wash my hands long enough, I secretly hid my dirty cuffs in the corner of the bathroom, I cleaned my shoes with white socks, and all that, measured by the demands of the little shirt, was hell for sure, everything that I did or wished for was bad. I searched through the cupboards for the Christmas presents, but I pretended I still believed that Jesus brought the presents when he visited us. This made my parents happy, I didn't want to be without that happiness. I hated flowers in vases because they wilted quickly and smelled bad, but I picked them in spite of that and gave them politely to Mama. I didn't like to go to the zoo, but I would pester them to take me there. Everything was wrong somehow, I couldn't really be what I truly am, they didn't allow me to. Perhaps childhood is often only a game, pretending to be a child for your parents, for teachers, for all grown-ups—not to cause them pain when something evil and already disfigured shows under the round, innocent face. Every upbringing maintains immaturity for a long time, that is its point. And we know very well what is expected of us, we make ourselves smaller because of it. We are malicious, crafty, obstinate, we take the slaps in the face with pleasure and become babies, tears flow and stop flowing, we do all this because we aren't permitted to grow.

My parents, weighed down with their everyday concerns, never did see through those rituals. Nor could they have, I was fiendishly careful in everything, as if I knew that I had to deceive them constantly, sitting on the floor, crying with a stupid teddy bear in my arms. I pinched the cat in passing, I fell down, I tore my dresses, I lied, I stole cookies, I secretly read pulp romances, I broke the teapot and didn't confess. All that corresponded to the picture of a child, and it was all the kind of bad deeds we commit because we're sitting in prison, on the playing field of the old-fashioned family that you deceive, that deceives you. Because they can't take you seriously either, because they too consider you a stupid kid, and they want to teach you how you should be, what you have to become someday, how you'll have to live someday, better than they did of course. Their life, yes, their mistakes. A child and parents—that is the epitome of a battle characterized by helplessness, because you have to play that child, otherwise you're lost. Otherwise they rush through all the rooms, all the gardens, pull you by the ears, by the pigtails, back into the house, into their room, where the stick they beat you with is waiting. The most underhanded bad deed is a lie. We know that we're lost without food and a bed, we know that we'd freeze outside alone and without them, that we don't yet know how to steal well, that the three-cornered eye still lives in our heads, in our ears the stories of how we'll burn if we dare to play with fire. We know that we're small and we can't find a job, and so we always return to mama again with a bowed head, we nag for a little pocket money, a gift, or a banana, we do what they expect of us. I didn't really want any of all the things I did, I did everything as it was prescribed, as it was expected, and so the little shirt with the little crosses got emptier and emptier until one day I finally threw it away. Growing up—it's a question of resistance, a question of power. I realized that late. I wanted to conform, and because of that I grew slowly.

■ □ ■ □ ■

II
OTHER TIMES

Mother

The body of recollection is a bee which stings me. It's not blood that bursts out through the skin of time, but upbringing and preparation for fear.

Today that old woman who shouts and curses at passersby was standing again on the balcony of the house on Kurfürstendamm. I think how good it is that Mama's not like that. Her misfortune is unmoving, mute, helpless. Her round, small body moves forlornly through the streets of Zagreb and buys bread and cheese at the market. But the rote performance of duty doesn't illuminate anything, doesn't give any kind of meaning. So the inconsolability of aging remained without crutches, they weren't provided to her, she didn't find them, she didn't know that one day a person needs them. Crutches are perseverance or prayer, or pleasure. An imprecise shame counterfeits the past, which lies around in rags, in cutouts. Because of that she hardly has any memory of it. She was born in 1902 in Travnik, it says on her christening certificate. In one picture she's with her sister in a sepia-colored garden in Mostar. A garden must have existed there, that was later, she was already twelve. Then her mother divorced her father, who worked in the Tobacco Administration. He was no longer a man to her after he took off the Austrian uniform he wore before their wedding. So she left Bosnia with her children, two girls and one boy, and returned to Vienna. They lived poorly in Vienna, on the charity of relatives. Both girls were placed in a convent boarding school. That's how Mama told it to me, when she talked about it. Nothing else exists. Her mother loved only her son. She reproached my mother for being like her father in everything. In the convent they always ate some awful porridge—it was during World War I—they wore black dresses, and in the morning she and her sister would have to break the ice in the basin so they could wash. They would kiss the doorknob some pretty nun had touched, and they were abandoned children, sacrificed to the institutions of the church and to other people's opinions. Because they alone know what is good, what is best. Did the sisters learn anything there? She can't tell me that. My mother doesn't know how to tell stories and is afraid of everything. It was surely awful there, dark rooms, prayers and whispering, stone floors, the coldness of ignorance. Later, at sixteen, she began working as a trainee at the Vienna Land Bank. Two years later her sister would do the same thing. She worked poorly, she had no clue about anything. But she was pretty, everyone flirted with her, and so she somehow got through those two years of training. Her sister made a career in the same bank and despised my incompetent mother all her life. Both gave all their earnings to their mother. In the evening all they ate was doughnuts with eggs and green salad. Anything they saved was spent on clothes. On the appearance that they were somewhat better, real ladies. Grandmother's upbringing, that appearance is the most important thing, would become the only ground my mother had to stand on. Her mother threw her first fiancé out of the apartment, in her opinion his feet stank. When she got home late after the movies with her second suitor, she was already twenty years old, the doors were locked and her pillow and blanket were lying outside.

She had to cry and beg to be let in, and she was not allowed ever to see the young man again.

On New Year's Eve in 1926 she fled with a small trunk to Belgrade to her girlfriend from the bank, she cried the whole night in the entirely empty train going into the unknown. Astonishing bravery, that escape. At first she lived with the girlfriend, but she quickly realized that her girlfriend was supported by men and that her house was a kind of brothel. She ran away to a furnished room and found a job at the Siemens office as a German-language secretary. She translated badly but everyone loved her, she was like some princess from Vienna. Every morning she found candies or chocolate on her desk. Since she knew that she hadn't really learned anything she once again had to count on her looks. She stepped lightly over the dirty cobblestones of the city in fine leather shoes with high heels. One day in a café she caught sight of my father, he was extremely good-looking, and she said to herself: This will be my great love. For the next few days she went to that café again—I see tables on the street, the soft sunlight, eyes full of hope—and they got acquainted. She was continually frightened by those beginnings of unlearned independence, she was confused amid the contradiction of child and woman. She was both, and each only by halves. She could not make a decision. But she wasn't hypocritical, she didn't refuse love before the wedding. Although she soon learned that he had tuberculosis and that he was probably deathly ill, things did come to a wedding. In the first year of the marriage she was very lonely, he was in a sanatorium on Klenovnik. The most beautiful love letters were written under the pressure of an imminent end. She still had nothing but them. Her mother couldn't forgive her for running away or for marrying some Balkan specimen. She decided that, if he remained alive, she would spend her whole life as his devoted nurse and would have no children.

But he returned from the sanatorium, he was no longer spitting blood, he no longer wanted to kill himself, as he had tried to twice. They found a little apartment, he made good money as an authorized clerk, she silently had several abortions. Once it was too late and so in 1930 she had her first child, me. She hoped: Everything will be fine. She left her job, happy to be rid of the nightmare of office life, and tried feverishly to learn the role of mother and housewife. She was uncertain, she had never cooked or sewn, I cried for months because she didn't know she had too little milk. My father said that her milk must be bad, he constantly shouted and it seemed to her that he was demonically superior to her in everything. Father went out every evening, she was alone at home. She had to find her paths in secret, had to avoid reproaches, had to be constantly on her guard. She played the role of seductress as clumsily as the role of housewife. She could count only on her beauty, she had nothing else. Resistance, independence, unfamiliar words. And he was always on her trail, he uncovered all her weaknesses. She covered up that torment with makeup and a permanent wave, she fought for at least the attention that young, attractive women get. Even then she already sensed the transience of her skin and was always somehow absent. Still, those first years were good, she wasn't afraid of me. Later, when I was often critical of her, she became strict. I didn't understand how she didn't have enough ground to stand on, and I constantly said things that she couldn't grasp. She couldn't hide her feelings and always took refuge in accidental outpourings of anger, in authority. It was a bad battle and didn't lead to anything. Father, who could have helped her, didn't do anything, he was raised the same way she was. So everything wound up in misunderstandings. She had lost her first, small independence, her dependence was expressed in shouting at the unimportant levels of the household. And so in that house, on the very bottom, she carried on her battles for new shoes, for us, for clothing, bed linen. At night those waves would calm down, but after several years even that was no longer possible. People say that love passes. But it was life that had passed, the one that means earning and spending, the dull circle couples move in, while they move under the invisible net of a land and a world they don't see, don't understand. It was always the same territorial battles for power and property. Books and newspapers weren't really read, the burden of middle-class marriage was not perceived. And therefore it was a life that passed so quickly, and later came only weariness, age, and nothing else. My father thought he had to fall in love again, she had to struggle, divorce meant defeat, what would other people say, how would she live. My sisters came into the world.

For a long time I had the feeling that my father was only a victim. I thought I understood his complaints that he couldn't have a conversation with her about anything anymore. Only much later did I become aware that these were the results of a narrow upbringing and his total lack of opportunity. But by then it was no longer possible to help, the wheels had already molded to the tracks of that life, bravery could no longer be awakened, no kind of stubbornness could be awakened any longer. Nothing existed but the wish to save, to hold on to at least something. They just shouted over every little thing, a meaningless scorn lay over everything. We children would escape into the dark corners of the apartment and from then on watch what was happening helplessly, maliciously. A brief truce reigned only during holidays. After 1945, when there were real problems with money, then all was lost. She tried again to work at the reception desk in a hotel where Father was the director, that can't have been good. Neither one knew how to talk about what troubled them. My father died of cancer at fifty-eight years of age, perhaps he didn't want any more, he solved all his problems, Mama was a widow. Without the dream of some other kind of future, from then on she searched for a substitute for the departed, and my sister Vera, who lived with her for ten years, took on that same role, his. Sickness, squabbles, the office. Vera would come home from work with the same expression on her face as my father, she fought the same battles, she uttered the same reproaches. She wanted to escape, to get married, it lasted ten years. When she went away to France with her husband we patched together Mother's life with visits, letters, gifts. And since she couldn't decide anything, we had to decide: what to cook, what to put on or read. Nothing genuine developed, we couldn't prevent the depressions that recurred. Drawn into unhappiness we made mistakes, we shouted, begged, but it was futile, the meaning of life could no longer be reestablished. The love we had felt, and which somehow became more and more unreal, was too weak: It is hard for two to live on a single strength. Digging around in the past brought only fear, only fragments, nonexistent consciousness was now the sole defense, and at the same time distress. And so that woman, who no longer has the strength for advice or aid, often sits alone in the room in Zagreb, she no longer wants to go out into the street, she says she feels like a stone. And that stone barely senses anything now, doesn't laugh, doesn't watch television, doesn't cry. Only sorrow remains, as she runs to the doctor, begging for pills, the ones that bring happiness or strength, so she can get up from her bed and play with her grandchildren.

The eternal sleep has already begun, and the redemption we fought for as if our own lives were at stake is not to be found. A hundred letters from us lie around the apartment, their brief aid is worthless. And so little parts of me too sit with her in the room, petrified, together we sip cold soup and stare into emptiness, at the fragments of a life from which one person once wanted to steal away with the help of a ghost. What we see, what we see too late, no longer helps. We have to live with that final defeat, look each other in the eye, and in the end close her eyes as well. Once I helplessly hit my head against the wall, Vera took great quantities of valerian drops in the bathroom, trembled and wept, the stone didn't budge. It didn't notice, the pains no longer penetrate to its core. Love is not pity; our parents' generation doesn't believe that, it doesn't recognize rebellious love.

When was that, the warmth of her hands on my shoulders?

Timelessness transforms everything into ice.

Kitchen Stories

Four women, three dwellings. Between them my dead father, a button from his winter coat in my sister Vera's pocket in spite of everything. I see dolls, scattered photographs, curls put away in boxes. I see the way I jumped on the bed for joy in 1940 when my father came into the room and said, "You have a little sister, but another one is on the way."

I sit in 1982 in Berlin, in the kitchen of some Chileans who had to flee after the putsch. I sit at Ingrid's and at Claudio's, and it's warm in the kitchen. We're all gathered around the little wooden table, wine and bread set before us, and our shadows gather on the wall. Here I have often received food and courage.

Those kitchens of our lives. No one ate lunch in the kitchen of my Zagreb childhood, in my memory it was always a closed, mysterious space, without any furniture. We ran into it only when we had to carry something into the dining room, and we would leave it immediately. No bread ever lay on its table—a table free of crumbs, empty and scrubbed clean. I no longer remember whether anyone ever cooked in that kitchen. Or did someone? Once I remember an old woman sitting there, holding a turkey between her legs. She opened his beak and stuffed him with macaroni. She took all the noodles from a big bowl and shoved them into him, so he would be fattened up by Christmas. The naked neck of the bird swelled up, the red veins spread endlessly. I was horribly afraid that his thin skin would burst. When did we eat that turkey? In 1943? In one photograph my sisters are sitting at a child-sized table, gnawing on greasy wings. They are three years old, they wear identical dresses, bows in their hair. The eaten turkey and its gnawed bones still lie in that kitchen, the loud shrieking and fluttering, while German airplanes drop tracer bombs, and their light penetrates the blacked-out balcony doors. The cold light of a bulb illuminates all those leftovers, greasy patches on the white tiles.

Later, when I got married, we had only one room and a bathroom on Bulić Street. You couldn't cook there, and we ate the food we brought home with us off our knees, sitting on a low couch. The refrigerator in the bathroom was almost always empty. I had a hard time tolerating that unity—the bathroom-toilet-larder—but the poverty of the first postwar years made that problem, which couldn't be solved anyway, easier for us. My sister Nada, when she came to Zagreb to study at twenty and was living in a little sublet room, also took baths in that bathroom. In that same tub my husband bathed with two women while I was working at the television station, and my neighbor reported it to me at once, she thought it was all terrible, more on account of morality than infidelity. To be in the tub in our bathroom-toilet-larder could be quite liberating, and so my sister tried her first flights too, her first settling of accounts with her sister. For a long time I wasn't suspicious of the pornographic pictures lying under the sink. In the morning I worked at the television station, in the afternoon he read us his love poetry, while I thought of the dress he had torn nine years ago and of how I had married him. But then there was also a kitchen I sat in as I do in Berlin. Every night in 1952 we sat on hard chairs at the home of the painter Stančić and his wife. They also had only one other room, their son slept in it. We talked about art, about food, no one had any money, Stančić ate

Maggi bullion cubes out of hunger, painted black pictures, showed us his pale body, the newspaper he wore between his body and his shirt to keep out the cold. The four of us loved each other as only forgotten people in an empty province can. It was snowing outside, drunks were singing in the bars. Z. and I read our first poems aloud, we published books in editions of seventy copies, the world was enormous and still undiscovered. We ate thick flour soups, that satisfied us, touch reigned, discussion, reconciliation. And that body, which the painter hated, blots of the skin and of the soul, heavy legs, the stories about poverty, his dreams—that was at last the life I had been searching for, which I found under the sickness and skin. The gentleness of that person with the prophetic traits, for whom outer appearance could offer no protection, the stories of mud and spiders in the low rooms of his childhood, the laments of a landless son of the village, pictures of the level expanse that trains raced through—all that inhabited the kitchen in Gajeva Street. I sat there every night for ten years. Afterward I was divorced. The Stančić family moved into their new apartment, now he was well known and prosperous, and from 1962 on we sat in a living room in soft yellow velvet armchairs, he could eat as much as he wanted. In 1977 he died, unrecognizably thin, outright skinny, he was fifty-one years old. The last evening I drank a whole bottle of whiskey and lied to him that he looked the same as ever. His esophagus, the aorta burst, the whole room was full of blood, that big and strong man bled to death, but the early longings from that kitchen were not fulfilled. Yet he sits with us now in the kitchen in Berlin, an unknown and uninvited guest, gets soup so he can satisfy his hunger. Once again no one has much money, it's warm, we find ourselves in the provinces just as we did long ago. He is still talking about the room that had one bed, on the wall a bright calendar with pictures of the Alps, and how that calendar was the most beautiful thing he saw as a child. Through the kitchen window in Berlin's Rothenburg Street I see a dark yard, the windows are different and somewhat higher than in Zagreb. At the same time I see nights in Homburg, I stand in Vera's kitchen, they've moved from France to Homburg. It's October, we have just arrived to visit her. In the kitchen there's a modern window that opens automatically, but outside that window dwells emptiness. An empty highway, standardized private one-story houses, gardens in which no children play, the neighbor's vicious dog, death. It was raining, the cars drove past eerily empty, in my sister's kitchen stands no round wooden table, friends don't come, she doesn't have any friends there. Vera pounded on the empty doors, ran around, called people, begged for someone to come. I said again, "Death in Homburg, no one comes." I stood by the window in her kitchen and thought: If you look any more into that night, you'll fall asleep, you'll become lifeless, beware. We lowered the blinds, Vera cooked us a fine dinner and so we forgot this Pirminius Street in Homburg. Perhaps we were no longer there, in that district of petty bourgeois prosperity, maybe we were wrong. The night is black, and we'll wake up in Zagreb, which Vera left eleven years ago. She got married and with her husband, a pharmeceutical company representative, she has come this far. Two sisters in Germany, times of migration, Vera lives near the highway, the ground she stands on is gray asphalt. In Zagreb she gave lessons to the old women who lived on the edge of town, taught them to read and write. But here in Homburg—she tells me this softly—cold blows through the walls, she sleeps with a cap over her eyes and ears, she freezes. Her twin sister Nada sits in Zagreb in her new and expensive kitchen, the first one she has ever owned, without her mother-in-law. Nada looks at the mechanics' garage down in the courtyard, smokes, translates thick books, the kitchen resounds with her typing. Green herb brandy in a cup, husband and children are asleep, there's a note on the side of the dish cabinet:

I'll drown in the swamp. Nada cuts women's heads, high flights of stairs, clouds out of newspapers and magazines and makes dark collages. She works at the Institute for the Preservation of Monuments, the decay of the cities is constant, her dreams are sad and childish. She turns the lights off very late.

The dead turkey cries in the night. In old, chipped, blue pots water boils without salt. Suspicion. The glass eye of the bird stares at us. Again I run out of the kitchen, everything repeats, the bursting naked neck, the veins, my fear. The nonexistent bread on that kitchen table is damp and sticky in recollection.

Nada and Vera

When my sisters were small, acquaintances would come to look at them, their similarity, their black eyes. I was eleven years old and was forgotten. But that didn't bother me because I was in love with them too. Besides that, it meant freedom for me; I would go to the Sava on my bicycle with the boys, we investigated all its channels, plunged into its depths and weren't at home for whole days. My sisters were seven years old when we were separated. Our parents moved with them to Opatija, where Papa took over a vacation hotel for medical workers. I was about to graduate from high school and stayed with acquaintances in Zagreb. We sold the piano, the bicycle, and I lived on that money. I couldn't go into my sublet room until nine at night, our acquaintance gave singing lessons in it, and since I didn't have money for the café I would freeze in the street until I was allowed to return.

I didn't see my sisters for five years. My parents lived with them in two hotel rooms, there was no place for me, they ate in the hotel dining room. When I came over for the first time with my fiancé, we paid my father for the food as if we were hotel guests. My sisters were twelve years old, they were happy, they were curious, our first books of poems were in print. But instead of two weeks we stayed only three days. Father was furious that Z. didn't wear a tie, that he had ugly hands, and that he greeted him quietly with his head bowed. Z. was working in a used-book store then, the dust from the old books ate up the skin on his hands. Papa went off to the beach with him, he called it: a conversation that should clear up a few points. They didn't come back for hours. Vera remembers how I cried and asked, "What would Papa do to him?" My sisters stood helplessly in the room and looked at me. The men came back late in the evening. Z. and I packed our bags and never went back to Opatija.

I saw my sisters again when they were nineteen years old. Nada means "hope," Vera means "faith." They didn't show any regret at our departure then, for fear of Papa.

Vera already had unhealthy lungs as a child, she would often miss school. Father would hit her when she got a fever, he thought she was getting sick because she didn't want to go to school. Out of fear she went on wetting the bed for a long time, and one of our mother's good deeds was to hide those sheets and secretly dry them. The Italian children in the school were against them, against the newcomers. After the establishment of the so-called B Zone, many Italians left Opatija, and then there were hardly any children left to play with. Vera fell behind a year in school, no one told Papa anything. When Vera was lying in a coma in the hospital, no one visited her. Some man killed their gray tomcat Dimo and told them he had eaten it. Nada experienced her first loves, Vera played the role of watchman in the park. Once when she was staying in Opatija alone they forgot to leave her coal and she almost froze to death.

At nineteen Nada came to study in Zagreb, Vera remained alone at the seashore. When Papa was in Vinogradska Hospital I exchanged those two hotel rooms for a small apartment in Zagreb, and that's how Mama and Vera came to Zagreb too. Papa never saw that apartment. Nada soon got married, took just one pillow and left the apartment, only Vera remained with Mama. After my divorce I gave them a little money each month, and I would come to have lunch with them. Vera worked at city hall, at the airport, at a bookkeeper's. Nothing was ever right. She went with Mama to the movies, on her annual vacation. A suicide attempt. In the hospital I poured tea into her by the quart. After that everything hung by a silken thread. She had to go in for a lung operation, I interrupted my fellowship in America. Six weeks in the hospital, intravenous feeding, I fainted when I saw her. That cold winter Stančić took coal to the apartment in taxis, Vera and I went to Venice alone, that was the agreement. And she began to fight. With my husband too. She took back the radio he had given me and had kept after the divorce, and she put it on the floor of the room on Bulić Street. But when we invited him to lunch one day my mother no longer understood this world.

My husband had gotten dreadfully weak then, he made a will, he didn't want a divorce. After the incident in the bathroom I remained firm. I quickly fell in love with a young painter, very jealous, and once when he wanted to break down the door of my apartment—I remember, I was peeling a hard-boiled egg—my neighbor, terrified by that noise, called Vera. She rushed over at once with my ex-husband, he wanted to beat up the young painter. Noisy quarrels, Vera was trembling, I laughed, he cried. We were restless, enchanted, and inconsolable.

Women's Stories

A cheerless landscape for women, that Croatian plain below Mount Sljeme, below a mountain that slides, that quakes and provokes fears. The men sit in the Old Roofs restaurant and eat lamb, drink murky white wine. The women are beasts of burden, mothers, and after a short time weary lovers. In families besides the ones like ours children are the sole gods. These children grow quickly and get stronger and stronger, especially the sons. After that they sit in old-fashioned cloth jackets in armchairs and sip Turkish coffee prepared by their wives. They like their mother's cooking best of all, they prefer to live on the street where they went to school, they're young for a long time and then suddenly old and tired, every year they want a new car, a different woman. A kind of dull physicality often hangs over everything here, dark rooms, dusty windows, unmade beds, curses. We didn't have an easy time with that. Like dolls we lost the lacquer from our cheeks, we threw our white kneesocks into the corners of our rooms, the silk bows, stiff collars. We wanted to be with them, to escape from our world, we wanted to live with those sons. We scraped the old photographs off the walls, we repainted our parents' green bedroom brown, we sat in basement apartments and were broken into everywhere. Things don't go so easily, and I learned that with difficulty and through banal details. My meteorologist cleans his teeth with his fingers, Vera said, and the story ended badly. My young suitor's hair smelled of sauerkraut, baked fish lay in his kitchen on newspapers and greased up the table, he thought that love was a sin, he ran to church, tormented himself. I got a stomach ulcer and we soon parted. Nada loved a young poet who drank and was missing his front teeth, her fiancé would wait for her night after night together with his mama. Before long they too got married and from then on lived as a threesome. When we visited her, her mother-in-law would walk quietly through the room in her bright housecoat, and we could never talk in privacy. A professor from Opatija wanted to marry my mother, but she always said that she didn't want to wash his socks. Then for the first time she got depressed. Vera made her wash the floor with a brush, for a little while she felt better, then even that didn't help anymore. One journalist from Belgrade got into the studio during a television rehearsal, offered me flowers, took the wedding ring off his finger, and announced that he wanted to marry me. The television personnel enjoyed that fiasco, I couldn't tell Mama and Vera because he was sitting there waiting for me, now he was courting Vera and Mama, writing me letters. I tore those letters up, Vera glued them back together, she thought it was a unique love story. Then someone else's turn came, he took pills so he wouldn't stutter. Stančić considered all of my boyfriends blockheads, especially the fat television journalist, who would get his revenge after many years and vote against giving me a job at the institution. Women's work, women's dependence. The facades of the houses peeled, the old porches smelled moldy, the new neon light was bright, every day and night the nearby tobacco factory spread its tobacco perfumes. Various cafés, dreams of happiness, the bad films of my youth, that whole slow life began to bother me, became physically alien to me. When Arno wanted to marry Vera and take her away to France, Mama cried and shouted: "Don't do it, you see how old I am." Vera shouted, grabbed me by the shoulders, cried loudly. I said, "Mama, jump off the balcony if you must, but she's going to marry Arno." The whole building heard that family nightmare, the evening was summer warm, and all the windows open. Thus shame entered the body too. Vera's wedding was in the church that looks like a Turkish steam bath, and they sped off for their honeymoon in a car with Mama and her trunks in the back seat. Later she moved to their place in France, but she couldn't stand it there, she didn't speak French, and quickly returned to the old apartment. From then on she would travel here and there, between Zagreb, Tours, and Berlin, leaving traces of unhappiness everywhere, hair combs, mute sorrow. That was no kind of life. Not for anyone.

On the deserted balcony in Zagreb, Vera's cactus plants bloomed like crazy even without her care. In time the walls of the room became gray and dusty, the railing rusted, the windowpanes became opaque, a home was lost. Stories about a family sit there, letters, coffins, lacquer from the mahogany. What lurks there is struggle, separation, a dark crack in the city landscape, lacerated skin, piled-up hatred. Mother, sisters, women! Save yourselves if you can!

Vera's Letter

. . . After a long time I'm sending you back the manuscript of your book about us. After our telephone conversation I sat down at the sewing table, put a typewriter on it, and began to write too. I didn't cook, I didn't clean up the apartment, I just wrote. I send you my stories even though it all seems too private to me since it's missing society, even the family. You remember me differently and that is a lot for a life which hasn't done anything significant for the community. Don't misunderstand me: Although I hope that I don't belong to the faceless masses, I'm still part of them in a way . . . Do what you like with my four stories. . . .

Vera

Story 1

"Italians in the middle, Serbs on the left, Croats on the right," said the teacher in the classroom. Nada and I stood on the left because we were born in Belgrade. After that Mladen didn't want to walk home with us anymore. Why? "Because I'm a proud Croat."—"And what does that mean?" Silence. We cried because he was our only friend.

At lunchtime in the hotel we talked about this with our parents. Papa almost tipped the table over in fury. "Not this again! You kids don't know anything! Your birthplace doesn't define your nationality! Shame on you! What stupid children I have! Get out of here!"

In the beginning there were seventy-three of us in the class in Opatija, and the war with the Italians was still raging. One day the room was almost empty. Where were the children? "They've gone back to Italy, now only Yugoslavs live here." "Ah, so, tell us Papa, are Yugoslavs Serbs or Croats or some third thing?"

Again Papa's fury, terrible fury: "Only you could be so stupid! What do you learn in school? Why do you go to school at all?"—"Us? We fight for a place to sit, we try to understand Italian and then to count. The teacher bangs his fist on the chalkboard when we're noisy, struggles with us. Papa, school is a struggle, but now it will be easier, now there will be more room, maybe we will finally even be able to sit down."

Story 2

Our room is cleaned up. We'll play with Irena when she gets here from Zagreb. We're happy. "Do you remember what she looks like?" I ask Nada. "Not really." "But she's our sister. Let's look for a picture of her so we'll recognize her."

"Why did Mama cry? That wedding, it will be something nice. We can't ask her anything. Papa doesn't talk to anyone anymore. Boy, he sure isn't glad."

"They're here! Quick! She's beautiful, he's very tall and so thin. She's little. Do you see his mustache?" "She just kissed us quickly and disappeared with him. But wait, I'm looking forward to lunch, it should be a real celebration."

Why can't we sit in the same room with them? We just look at them through the door. They're very serious. The lunch isn't a celebration, Irena's crying. Oh, she's paying for lunch, are they crazy? Where is Papa going with her fiancé?

It's evening. Papa's not back yet. Has he killed Irena's fiancé? Here they are, they're coming. They're both furious, now Mama is crying too. I'm never going to get married. If we play with Irena will she maybe forget about the wedding?

What? They're already leaving? We didn't even get to play

with her. Mama is crying. Irena's not crying anymore. Her fiancé is calming her down. How can a person be so thin? "Come here, let's look for something sweet to give him."

We don't have any candy, there's nothing in the room. They're already leaving. Irena says she'll never come back again. Everything is over, they've gone. What a quarrel in the house. Mama is beside herself: "I don't want to lose my child." Does she really think that if Irena never comes back again, she's lost her for good? I don't want to run into Papa. He's mean when he's so angry. I'll never get married. I'll never see Irena again. Now I'm crying too. I wanted to play with her, I wanted her to write something in my album. "You know, they write poems, her fiancé too." "I'm sure Papa won't read them." He doesn't read poetry. He only works and scolds people.

Story 3

"That's nice, if you're looking for fifteen office workers, then there'll be a place for me." And so I went to city hall. "What experience do you have? Do you have a high school diploma? Good, you have to begin at the beginning, in the archives."

So I got my first job. Behind a glass partition, in the registry office, constantly going up amd down ladders with heavy bundles of papers. A job in the dust, in the basement, in a draft.

Irena got divorced from Z. after an unfortunate incident, Nada got married, it was as if my mother was lost, often depressed. I was tired most of the time, I would work with a fever so my small salary wouldn't shrink even further. Irena gave her husband the keys to the apartment, so he could take his things. When they divided up the things, Irena made their last coal payments, and he didn't have any money to pay her back. "I won't allow it," I told Irena and began to follow him everywhere—because of that money for the coal and because of some other things.

By the time I found out with difficulty where Nada lived and *who her husband was, she was already pregnant and I didn't want burden her with problems. I never asked why she got married secretly. My job got to be too tiring and I began look-ing for another one. I had trouble finding my ex-brother-in-law. My illnesses piled up, I was always tired. After a telephone argument, Z. promised me he would pay for the coal. At nine o'clock in the evening he paid me a hundred thousand dinars on the street. He licked his fingertips and counted the bills, people looked at us, the wind was blowing and I was afraid that the bills would fly away from me. I'll never forget that dark street, that money counting, and the people. But my weak knees didn't give way. He also asked me about Nada's child and then left me on the empty street.*

I found a new job at the airport. Getting up at five, working until eleven at night the next day. Doing that every other day. Fatigue and illness. I constantly had a fever, the medi-cine no longer helped.

Mama was desperate, she couldn't help. "Weak people are condemned ahead of time . . ." rang in my ears, I thought that Papa was right, and I decided to die. In the cornfield by the airport no one would ever find me, I drank the poison, scribbled a few words to Mama, quickly washed out the cup, and went out into the field.

When I came to, Irena was standing beside my bed repeating, "Drink a little more tea, please drink." I hadn't thought of her. But she was standing beside me, not asking me anything.

Story 4

The flooding in the city was more severe than people thought. I was working at the Ministry of Health and we organized help for the flooded area. I took part in the relief drive too, in a rubber boat rowed by one of the soldiers. "Row further, further still, please, there to the left, further." He didn't want to row anymore, there were no more houses, the cur-rent was strong. "Further," I yelled, "further." And then I caught sight of people calling for help up in a tree. It was a whole family, the parents and two children. "How did you find us?" they asked. "No one else came this far, we've been waiting two days and two nights." The children weren't crying, they were just hungry and frightened. I was happy, the soldier was happy too. But those people, so far outside the city, whose lives we saved—it was hard to understand. Something forced me to keep rowing and to this day I can't explain what kept me going.

Of course I got sick again, all this was too strenuous for me. The doctor didn't want to come over anymore, he said on the telephone, "I can't help you this way anymore, send your mother, I'll give her the medicine." I was alone at home when I heard a ring at the door. I could tell right away from the heavy breathing who it was. Stančić had climbed the four floors to our apartment in order to find Irena. He was always looking for her. My paleness kept him from leaving right away. "How can I cheer you up, tell me, I'll do anything, just smile. Spring will be here soon."

I smiled and said, "Paint my portrait." He was a famous painter.

"Come over tomorrow, I'll paint you," he said, and left. It's now or never, I thought. And the next day I went to his place with a fever. He was very careful, he was worried, he took care not to tire me and always listened to the same Katarina Valenta record while he was painting. He worked unbelievably fast. I was in his studio twice and the painting was almost ready. I saw myself in that portrait, recognized me. I wanted to hug him, but he was so big, so fat that it wasn't possible.

After that we stopped working for a few days so I could get better, so my fever would come down. Suddenly his wife called me: "Vera, come over, Miljenko might sell your portrait."

I went to see her right away and she gave me the painting, still wet. I carried that picture, myself, home through the city. Irena took a look at it and said, "It's you, Vera."

THE SILK, THE SHEARS

Nada's Letter: Long Ago

Zagreb? Only a couple of pictures remain in my memory. A very fat woman with a wide lap, stuffing the turkey she held, shoving dumplings into its beak and forcing them through its long neck with her hands. I can't see her face, I see only the broad lap, the turkey's long neck and its eyes.

The clatter of wooden clogs. The boys who chase us banging their clogs in their hands while we return from school in the evening on Pantovčak, heading for the shacks. We run as fast as our legs can go. They catch Vera. I run away horrified. Vera manages to free herself, and then Papa comes into the street. Mama darns socks under a lamp in some undefined corner between the wooden walls of the shack. I don't remember leaving. In Opatija, in the huge and deserted half-destroyed hotel building, we can't sleep because of the sound of the sea. It's damp and gray. A lot of rain falls. The city is, so to speak, empty. I'm afraid of the dark. I'm afraid to be alone. At night I see ghosts, I hear steps, I strain my ears to hear the clicking of a lock and the opening of a door. I pull the covers over my head and shake with fear. For days. For years.

Only later, when I am withdrawing more and more into myself, when I want desperately to play the piano, I become brave and in spite of everything, trembling, enter the hall with the piano in the completely empty hotel building. Tables and chairs are stacked in piles. There's no one anywhere, the hotel isn't open in the winter. I go to play regularly and try to learn from the music I get from a friend. I get an F in sightsinging in school. The nervous director constantly spits on us while he yells and directs how we should sing. He is old and very gray. I don't remember him ever cracking a smile.

In the big hotel park, our house in a clump of laurels. A little secret entrance. Split logs inside. The two of us and a few friends hide in here, pretending that it's our house. They don't find us there for a long time.

At home I keep an ear posted in fear; will Father come home from work and summon me? Endless sitting in the armchair while he sleeps, leaning on me. I'm stiff with pain, I don't dare to budge so as not to wake him. At least he leaves me in peace while he sleeps. I don't know where Mama is. I don't like her soft, absent touch. I'm panic-stricken by Father's touch, possessive, imposed, frightening, male, and distracted. The smell of his hair bothers me. I remember it to this day. To this day every hand laid on me makes me remove it, get rid of it.

Through the rain, without an umbrella, with the then-typical Weltschmerz in my heart, I wander around the city and dream of James Dean. I don't have the courage to run away. I don't have the courage for anything. Fear planted in my bones. Such fear that it's possible to think: Papa will take a knife and kill Vera, or me, or Mama, do something horrible, if everything isn't the way he has decreed. The same fear in all of us. Irena shouts and throws herself on the couch, kicks her feet up in the air out of despair because he has gone for a walk with her fiancé. It's all a vicious cycle of senseless fear.

After I finish high school Father gets me a job in some hotel in Lovran. A college of medicine has opened in Rijeka and he wants to enroll me there. I go to some classes. The big modern building fascinates me, the hall with the amphitheater, the new shining seats. I faint when they show a film about an operation. I leave, certain that this will never be my vocation. As if in a dream, as if led by some secret force of the subconscious or the unconscious, Mama helps me to register clandestinely at the university in Zagreb, in the art history department. She finds me a room to sublet too. With the train ticket already in my hand we reveal the secret to Papa. In my frightened excitement, in the whirl of guesses, I don't remember at all how I left, I don't remember the train, the trunks, not a thing.

Zagreb again. I don't recognize it at all. Fortunately, I live on the street where we lived ten years ago. It is familiar to me. I often pass our former house, where we lived on the second floor, and ponder how nice it would be if we had stayed there. On the street no one looks familiar anymore.

My sublet room is next to the kitchen. It's a cramped girl's room with an old wardrobe, a bed, and a chair. I come home only in the evening. When I turn on the light in the kitchen, cockroaches scurry off in all directions. I'm desperate. I block up all the openings in the door with newspaper so the cockroaches can't get into the room. I do this every evening, but the occasional cockroach still manages to get into the room. I can't sleep from horror in that small space where there's no room to move except in bed.

Papa is already in a hospital in Zagreb. Every day I go see him out of fear, because what would he say if I didn't go? He governs me even when he's immobile. The smell of his room is ugly. It creeps under my skin. Every time I go, a forced kiss on the face swollen from disease, which stinks of medicines and sedatives unknown to me. Repulsion. Sorrow. Pity. More than pity, there is the desire for all this to end as soon as possible. My sisters don't want to wash his things, especially the handkerchiefs. He's covered in sores, everything is rotting before our eyes, but life doesn't give up. Now he's nonetheless pleased with my studies. He wants me to talk to him about art. He offers me cigarettes. In my little room I secretly boil my father's handkerchiefs and sometimes his pajamas at night in an UNRA can on a little electric hotplate. I do all this in secret. In the kitchen the milk boiled down until the pan turned black. In my fear that someone might see me boiling linen I forget about the milk.

Some days I eat only one meat pie a day. I buy two or three cigarettes, never a whole pack. When they are smoked the butts left over in the ashtray are lit again. It doesn't matter who smoked them. In the club, at school, in the evening we sit a long time and smoke. We listen to music and talk. We discuss art. We're entirely possessed by surrealism and dadaism. The poems of Henri Michaux, André Breton. At Fanika's we drink mulled wine. Irena and Zvonko have a par-

ticular influence on me. I find a temple of art in their little efficiency apartment. Numberless books, little Negro sculptures, Stančić's pictures on the wall. Books, poems, books. As if I had entered a whole new world. I'm always afraid that I'm an alien there, a necessary evil, a part of the family who's not loved and not needed. Imposed by the force of nature and not a friend of one's own choice. For years I will strive to win over Irena's friendship, for years I will regret that I don't feel her interest in my life and being as anything other than interest in a younger sister. I probably judged her unfairly. But when she spoke about other people, about their problems, their fates, their quality of soul and heart, I always longed for her to see me and understand me that way. For her to introduce me simply: This is Nada— or to say: This is my Nada, I longed for that word my *to have full significance, I did not want to hear her say: This is my sister. I didn't want to be a sister, or a daughter, I didn't want any kind of connection imposed on me. I wanted only to be myself. Without anyone else. Only I and as such sufficient for love and friendship to some other. And that other could have been anyone—sister, brother-in-law, friend, husband, it didn't matter. Only rarely have I managed to achieve this.*

Father 1

For what sort of contents were we three daughters supposed to be the vessel?

What I see, recognize, isn't a refuge. The child's body is a perforated target which rain, upbringing, and arrogance pass through.

Like a spirit level I float at a single point above that swamp, I look at the remnants of milky hot cereal, of pillows hot from fever. And the pictures are a flight from content. They are saturated in a horrible way. The liberated root shows its whitish notches—fine society has slashed at it.

THE SILK, THE SHEARS

Under the photograph in the family album where I'm a nine-month-old baby running toward Mama, it says in Papa's handwriting: "First steps. Finally. All that is great takes time." Those were notions, goals. Their poison in the spirit—our beds of consciousness. Their red pencil crossed out in our library all the testimonies of the defeated, all hunger and torment.

Once Papa and I were lying on the floor on both sides of the double bed and rolling a split log like a ball. I was three years old, the log hit me on the head. Later they lied to me and said that the maid dropped me on the balcony and that was where the scar on my forehead comes from. A candle was fastened to one end of my little yellow toy walking stick. Father used it to light the highest candles up on the Christmas tree. The rest of the year he would hit me with it because I didn't want to eat or sleep. In the afternoon I always lay on the couch with Papa and for months he would tell me stories in installments—about a dog that everyone chases away—and I would cry. After that he began reading his melancholy poems aloud. I was always afraid of him, but I was also proud, for he read the poems to me and not to other people. Days, years go by. Blows, literature, milky hot cereal. I never saw my parents naked, for a long time I believed in the stork. Father came home from the office with his eternal expression of suffering, he was silent, he got the biggest piece of meat at lunch. I felt that burden of his clearly— he was working for us. If he would just look at me, I would go pale, once when he threw all the plates on the floor together with the tablecloth I got hysterical and was hit again, for two days I couldn't walk. Mother told me that for the first year of my life he didn't even want to look at me— he thought that my diapers stank and that I was boring. When I was twelve I didn't get any Christmas presents, instead I got a letter from him, twenty-four pages long. In the letter he wrote that now that I was a grown-up girl, it was time for me to stop getting childish presents, that I must be orderly, kind to my parents, that I must know that a person doesn't have many friends in life, that that's how it is, and that parents, well, they have their own lives, their own cares. He poured onto me all his bitterness, all his hatred of the world, early on he drew future disillusionments on all the walls around me and said: Everything will surely happen to you that way. I wasn't allowed to be a child, I had to read Dostoyevsky's *Idiot* and tell him the contents. Most of the time I would tell him too briefly and he would yell for hours that I was as stupid as my sisters, as stupid as Mama, as stupid as everyone else. He tormented me with arithmetic, he sat beside me with a watch while I practiced on the piano, I had to read books about yoga, Spengler's *Decline of the West*, Friedell's *Cultural History of the Modern Age*. And so I quickly learned various tricks, odd answers that covered up the emptiness of my knowledge. I got him going about the moon or stars, he would fall into that trap, he forgot about his questions and for hours talked to me about the universe.

I couldn't ask anything real at that time. Reality awoke anger in him, it was that scorn of the half-educated, that appearance of knowledge, substitute, senseless stories which don't bring anything. All was mere quibbling. So I haul the traces of endless sentences through rooms, corridors, gardens, I clench a fist, I dig my nails into the flesh to feel that something really exists. When I fell in love with Miran he threw him out of the apartment. He said: He has the nose of a heart patient and the handwriting of a thief. He would punish me for the littlest things by grounding me from the movies for a year. I had to visit a Franciscan with him and listen to discussions about whether God exists. I had to dance with him even though I hated it. He showed me off to others and I had to be smart, pretty, *his* daughter. They removed the polyps from my nose without anesthesia, he held me on his lap: That's how you're supposed to bear things. He himself wanted his teeth pulled without anesthesia, once he passed out at the dentist's. He had depressions, suicidal thoughts, bilious attacks, pains in his stomach, intestinal colic. Theoretically many things could happen to him, but at the same time outpourings of fury lurked inside. It was as if he had a black cavern inside him. During the war he played poker and lost, he had a way of disappearing at night into bars. When we wound up with no money he became a real socialist, he worked devotedly day and night, he no longer had the need for a nice apartment, for white tablecloths, he no longer wrote poems. He saved the young cook of the resort from dying—for he just knew something had happened to her (she almost bled to death), since she wasn't in the kitchen. He looked for her everywhere and got her to the hospital in the nick of time. He was visited by feelings which he hadn't had for his own family for a long time.

For nine months in 1960 I went to see him every day in the hospital in Zagreb, Mother and Vera were still in Opatija. He had cancer of the epipharynx, they diagnosed it too late, they radiated him with a cobalt bomb. He suffered terribly, his bones were already full of holes, and once he broke his arm when he was turning over. I washed him as Nada did, changed his clothes, his body was full of swellings. I bought kerosene for him because he had read that a woman had once cured herself with it, I fed him a pint of it every day with a spoon and then fed him an orange to clear away the stale taste. Superstitions, hopes, struggle. For a few days he even got better from this treatment, he got up from his bed and waited for me in the hospital garden, he was fifty-eight years old.

My husband and I had a small fisherman's cottage in Rovinj. Z. was at the shore at that time. At the end of August the doctor told me that I should go on vacation too, that things with Papa could go on for months. I had been in Rovinj for two days when the telegram came announcing Papa's death. Z. refused to come back to Zagreb with me, he hated funerals. I rode for hours in a stuffy bus and felt abandoned, weak. Later I found out that Z. had met with his lovers in our house in Rovinj. An acquaintance, a red-haired singer, attacked him for doing that in front of our house and from then on she wouldn't speak to him anymore. I saw her only twice more, she wasn't singing anymore, she was ill, she got a blockage of the intestine and died.

Our mother had a black veil across her face in the baking sun and after the funeral she stood for hours in the hall stroking Father's winter coat, which they had brought from the hospital along with his suit and umbrella. Nada wore black in mourning for a long time, a show of loss went on a long time. Mama was unhappy, the sufferings of the married years were forgotten, there was no kind of recollection. Vera had to promise that she would never desert her. Loneliness is a death sentence for children—women. It took three months before I could cry: It's incomprehensible that he's no longer speaking, looking, that he's gone. Loss takes on new meanings, I don't regret that we've lost him, I'm sorry that he can't see us anymore, our lives, that he can no longer find out anything else or change anything. That ultimate death of consciousness, that impossibility of change, that loss of all experiences, that for me was death. Now I would like to talk with him, ask him, tell him about us, but he got away from us, he had to leave and sometimes it seems to me that he was glad to do it.

The silver ornaments on the Christmas tree break under the blows of a child's yellow walking stick. Renunciation of reality, of conversations about it, because now it is suddenly too late, that was the wooden clerk's coffin he lay in with his fury, his pains, and his strictness. It is irrevocably so, because of that I cried. And I felt that what is written in hell is also a form of knowledge, for tenderness can spring up everywhere. Stale fears pale through writing and grow smaller.

Family Proverbs

Hunchbacks bring misfortune. Time is money. The Moor has done his duty. The first kittens get thrown into the water. Crockery fragments bring happiness, a broken mirror brings seven years of bad luck. Homo homini lupus. Not all that glitters is gold. Pearls mean tears. The way to a man's heart is through his stomach. Evil is in the way of things. One swallow does not make a spring. Gypsies steal chickens and children who are naughty. A spider seen in the morning brings worry. Per aspera ad astra. Miracles don't exist. He who works also sins. He who flies high falls low. The path to you leads around the world. Still waters tear the banks. Long on hair, short on brains. To each his own. Money alone doesn't bring satisfaction. Don't wake a sleeping lion. Life is serious, art is cheerful. Better a sparrow in the hand than a dove on the roof. No one walks under the palms unpunished. Everyone is the forger of his own happiness. Dreams are made of foam. Misfortunes never come alone. Everything on the table must be eaten. A lie has short legs. Tomorrow, tomorrow, never today, that's what lazy people say. He who laughs last laughs best. The one who beats you is the one who loves you. The trees are flourishing that will build our coffins. A liar has a very soft-tipped nose. Man is alone in life. Laziness stinks. The one who punishes you wishes you all the best.

And so forth.

The Microscope

During the war Grandfather got in touch with us—the one who had taken off his Austrian uniform in Bosnia. Mama's papa lived in retirement in Zagreb, he began visiting us, he always came alone. So we didn't know for a long time that he was hiding a friend in his apartment, a Jewish woman. They had met right before the war at the movies, she was a widow. Grandfather risked his life saving Vinka's life and he was a quiet man. Mama found him after many years, but he didn't become a father to her, she didn't dare ask why he had never taken care of his children. When Grandfather died we went on visiting Aunt Vinka, today she's ninety years old, she can't walk and we bring her fish from the market, she likes them.

From the age of thirteen I had a friend on our street, Nina, we often played in her garden with the white outdoor furniture. An old woman lived in the basement of the building with her two nephews. Both of them were studying medicine, and when they had time they would play table tennis with us behind the house. Sometimes one of them, Vlado, would sit at the white table in the garden. His thick books lay on the table, a microscope and a collection of glass slides. He was studying for an exam and one of the books was called *Pathology*. I could take a look through the microscope at the causes of various diseases, and besides a sharp serve, Vlado taught me many things about the spiral creatures in the blood of sick people.

And so every day I went off to the garden, I was in love with Vlado. He was nineteen years old and had a girlfriend who came over every evening. I hated her. She wore lots of make-up, she was stylishly dressed, they would go out together to the movies or dancing. Vlado must have noticed quickly that I was in love. Once, on the steps to the basement, he gave me a kiss in passing. I stood there frozen like a statue, I almost fainted from happiness, I ran onto the street and back again into the garden, I gave Nina a wild hug. But from that day on Vlado no longer sat in the garden with his books, I waited for him in vain. I slunk around the house, I peered into the low windows, I stood alone with a paddle at the green Ping-Pong table. I was unhappy.

A month later Vlado sent me a letter. I had to promise that I would tear the letter up after reading it, later I did so. I opened it with trembling hands in our garden under the low kitchen balcony. I didn't entirely understand the letter. It was really beautiful, his tiny handwriting, and there was something in it about the impossibility of love for a child and how he himself didn't understand that something like that could happen to him, and that he couldn't see me anymore. I suffered a long time and hoped for a long time that I'd manage to grow up quickly, and that I'd go to him, throw his girlfriend out of the apartment, and stay with him. He soon moved away from his aunt's and I didn't see him until many years later, in a crowded streetcar on Ilica Avenue. He was as gentle as before, now he was a well-known specialist in children's diseases and married. But not to that made-up woman, I asked him that.

Then, when I didn't see Vlado anymore, I began to study ballet like crazy, I tried to fall in love, but I couldn't, and for a good five years I didn't feel like it. Then Papa put a stop to the dancing because I would have to give up school if ballet was to be a main interest for me. I agreed to give up ballet without a struggle, I wasn't regretful, I constantly thought only of the garden, of the wooden table, pathology, and the way Vlado would place my head above the lens so I could see the typhus germs better. I knew many things then from his thick book, I had read what was underlined in red pencil, and I wanted to become a doctor. Or a table tennis player. I would have stayed with him in the basement at his aunt's but I was too little, it was too early. When I was still sixteen I looked for him among the students coming down the steps from the Šalata Clinic, once I even stood at the door of his aunt's apartment, but I didn't ring the doorbell.

Somehow I knew that he couldn't wait until I grew up, but maybe it was a mistake that I didn't ring the doorbell and ask where he lived. I also knew that he was very poor. His wife is probably very rich, I do suspect that, but since I didn't possess anything then—now I sense it—maybe that's why I didn't ring the bell. I knew he would have found me already if he had believed that the road from poverty to being a well-known doctor was possible despite the burden of a girl without a winter coat. When I meet him again I'll ask him whether he didn't have the courage for it then, whether he was afraid, and whether he married a wealthy woman. Vlado O., why has that doubt occured to me now? The causes of diseases under the microscope lens are tinted reddish and signify danger, the garden suddenly shrinks, the furniture loses its color, the white oil paint peels off. Once again I'm sitting there with you and studying your face. But you don't look at me, you evade the childish questions. The microscope now enlarges everything: heart, reason, memory. You escaped from that garden; was that pathology, or just some kind of calculation? Now I'm uncertain, the garden gate loudly closes and opens, your aunt goes off to market in a black coat. She shouts at you, I remember now, there's no money for meat. Your pants were worn, your girlfriend had a fur coat on, she was much older than you: No, you didn't love her. The thick book is closed on the table. The girlfriend was often in a bad mood, dissatisfied, she wasn't sure of you. She didn't like me either, there was too much fear in the game. Did you sacrifice a future together under the burden of poverty? Were you as mild and weak as I already felt as a child? And I wanted to protect you, I was ready to learn all of pathology by heart so as to prepare for the exam with you. Was your light, supple walk, which I loved, only a reflection of your readiness to run away?

Once again I'm thirteen years old and I ask you, do you want the apple or the sandwich I've brought? It's chilly, we sit in the garden, you eat and are silent. You just eat and keep silent. And that could be a parting after so many years.

Old Pigtails

At fifteen I cut off my pigtails, I cut my hair short and it quickly darkened. The halls of our high school stank of disinfectant, the floors were varnished with dark brown grease. We all wore the prescribed school uniforms, mine was indigo with a round white collar and white buttons. Most of the children came from Zagreb and vicinity, I was the smallest in the class and for me the other girls were already women. The first boyfriends waited for some of the girls in front of the school, in class they secretly put lipstick on and left proudly with the guys for the nearby park on Marulić Square. I went home alone, I carried my heavy bag and thought that there would be time for dating someday. But even later no one waited for me in front of the school, it was something I never had any success at, and it was an important thing, a matter of prestige. For a short time I considered taking part in the race, but it seemed to me that I didn't have to. In school we learned everything without question. We learned greedily, like all postwar children—knowing something meant power. The class was big, the teacher didn't teach mathematics methodically, she was liberal with our grades, all the girls got their diplomas, all went on to the university.

At home Papa would ask: Have you already told her? And Mama would nod her head. He was in fact asking whether she had explained to me how babies are made, but she could not tell me and she never did. Later Papa would say: If something happens, don't do anything stupid but come home to us, we'll put everything in order. I was calm even though at seventeen I still didn't understand what he was hinting at. I accepted the language of my parents, which covered secrets and all that was unsaid, without question, without curiosity. It was all meant to be that way anyway, I made peace with it,

I caught on early to the fact that they couldn't talk about real problems. Sometimes I was amazed at how I was born at all from that maidenish, aseptic mother, that father, so anxious. I recall that even as a small child I was terribly ashamed when they would kiss good-bye at the train station. It was so unpleasant for me that I would move away from them and act as if I didn't know them. Maybe it was because I had never seen them do it at home. But why then in public? I was angry and full of shame. And so puberty came as a surprise. I felt out of season, I cried at every little thing. And when one Sunday Papa slammed the door and furiously left the apartment, Mother and I were standing in the middle room, I yelled at her: It's your fault he's leaving us forever. Mother calmly slapped me. A quarrel, slamming doors, a slap. The sun shone through the open windows into the room, the bells rang with holiday stupidity, and I was suddenly sick of everything, I rushed off to our balcony and wanted to jump off. Pointless at that height. I was beside myself, everything hurt me, I didn't want to know anything anymore, I wanted to disappear. I don't know who held me back and calmed me down, but for a long time I avoided Mama. I thought she was to blame for everything, I cried secretly at night.

In school I sat next to Djurdja, once again I was in love with the biology teacher, I gave a report on tropical diseases, I went off secretly to the university and listened to lectures on forensic medicine. I read all the Russian novels, Goncharov's *Precipice* two times, I read one book a day. While reading I would eat cookies and I put on weight. I talked with Neda in the park in front of school about her father's mistress, with Maja about the partisan school where she had been during the war, with Vera Kružić about Gracián's prophecy. With Djurdja I wrote letters to an unknown poet while her boyfriend announced his arrival by loudly revving up his motorcycle outside the window. Her parents had hand-picked him, at that time we hadn't really noticed him. He didn't read poetry, he was in love with technology. All we wanted was to stay together, to read and write, to converse about art. Girls' dreams are ephemeral, later Djurdja married him, he is very sweet and good, they still have that old grape arbor from our childhood, and when I visited her not long ago in her new house she was glad and at the same time suspicious because of my long absence. All the same, we could talk just like long ago: At first I didn't dare mention the past, it never meant that we would have a future together, I am aware of that. My uncertain life didn't strike her as especially successful, at one time I was the best student in the school, and everyone went on to the university. I didn't get any sort of degree and that's a weakness, no kind of perseverance, none, by any means. She said to me again, "My life is surely uninteresting to you," old fears, while I said, "If we keep on doubting for a long time, then everything truly will pass away, that past time of ours, the high beds in your parents' house, warm homemade bread, grapes in the orchard, your mother's hands as she tucked us in before she left the house and left us walnuts and honey on the bedside cabinet." I tell her that we don't need a country house. For a long time she has been working in a factory laboratory. On Sundays friends roast good meat in the garden, sing, dance. Once she found a similar house for us and we went off to see it, a person could really weaken. The house overgrown with ivy, a pretty round tile stove in the room, the garden dark with fruit trees. When I say it won't do, it's too expensive, then maybe she thinks that I don't want to live in the same place, maybe she thinks that I don't like her, that I'm a well-known writer now and that her life doesn't interest me. And everything always turns out that way, and she hasn't found total peace either in the house they have built, she works too much. And so now I bring a friend to see her, his brother works for Siemens in Berlin, he's looking for a weekend house, we still haven't found anything for him, the reasons are complicated. Djurdja bakes beautiful cookies for us, takes care of everyone, takes workers by bus to the theater in Zagreb, reads until late at night, hugs me passionately. These are our dreams, half-dreams, an equality like a utopia, that eternal: no, nothing, yes, everything. I no longer need as much consolation from words, the world seems forlorn to me in a different way, we don't hold on to the horror that approaches inside ourselves, I know that. Despite that, let it come to us anonymously and without a roof over our heads, that roof that my family believed in, if it is possible. No, nothing will be left, no pages covered with poems, no houses, success, or other signs of power. She has a daughter, she wants that kind of security for her, I know that, all the reasons are understandable. The dolls on her bed are a decoration and a tender memory, she has long sensed that my handshake is too weak, school days were a dream of youth and my absence a horrible betrayal. You stand there with one trunk after years of work and many people avoid you. But even that trunk is still too much, still too heavy. My feeling about the trunk, I'd like to explain it. But I rarely manage to explain it, everything looks like an attack or like envy. That's not what I want anymore. And so sometimes we are silent. Different girls sit on the benches in the park, the sentences are a bit dull, they are colonized by veils of grayness.

We can't just remain the way we are in a belly full of reminiscences, that too is torn apart, ripped apart, something always leads beyond that refuge, leads over the ramp of our childhood, and outside it's cold or it's not cold. But not only the past makes up our minds. And unforgettable classmates are eternal in some sure way.

Spring

In May of 1945 partisans in torn uniforms and wrapped feet sit in the garden of the house in Buconjić Street. Their rifles lean against the fence and aim down the steep street. Mama

THE SILK, THE SHEARS

57

brews tea for them in our kitchen in a big pot, we children throw packs of cigarettes through the window into the garden. We don't have go to school, I don't have to practice the piano, holidays.

Papa thinks that they'll interrogate him, he has already packed a small trunk. He thinks this because of his job at the Boehler firm, so he stays home for several days. Mama teases him about it, though she doesn't know what's going on either. Then all at once we have six subtenants in the apartment. The five of us get one room, Papa's mama, who is suddenly here, gets the girls' room, the subtenants get the other rooms. We sleep in a crowd, lines form outside the bathroom. The daughter of the deported Šlezinger family moves in above us, she wears a partisan uniform. The colonel who collaborated with the Germans has disappeared.

Granules of memory sit in me as if in a ripe rosehip. Pictures. Since Mama has blond hair, Papa thinks that she shouldn't go out and so she is constantly at home. We don't speak German and I don't understand anything anymore. Papa doesn't work, a friend gives him some money and says, "Every time I slept at your apartment, the Gestapo was looking for me at my place." The woman commissar who lives in the dining room looks suspiciously at the furniture, the oil paintings, us. Instead of looking for a smaller apartment Papa wants to stay here. In order to survive we sell almost everything we have: the sewing machine, the porcelain, carpets, books, the black, lacquered furniture. I go to the Eighth Girls' High School on Roosevelt Square, it's the era of my friendship with Djurjda. Before the start of school I go to lessons for the girls who were in partisan schools, I'm never at home, I don't have one anymore. Djurjda lives in a little house on Trešnjevka, we study together, we sit in the garden, I can sleep at her place, no one asks where I am, the family has other concerns. Djurjda didn't like to speak with the other girls in the class, she gave me dried flowers, sent letters and telegrams. Once when I visited Neda she didn't want to talk with me anymore, she gave me back my picture, then we quickly made peace. In school we learned about the war that had just ended, history. I was like blotting paper that soaks everything in, greedy for everything that was different, rough, earthy, avid for another world.

When Father told the commissar that she couldn't have visitors, after all he had three daughters—ah yes, that same old morality—then we quickly lost the apartment. The remnants of the furniture were loaded onto a truck and the drive led into a suburb to a settlement of shacks. We got two rooms with a kitchen in one of them. Wooden floors, cold, the toilet was always dirty, wooden boards lay outside the doors because of the mud. We carried water from the pump along with the others. With drunks, enemies, transients. Papa's face turned gray. Grandmother took a knife and tried to stab herself. She was taken off to the asylum, my parents moved away to Opatija with my sisters.

I remained in Zagreb, my straight A's guaranteed me a high school diploma. I didn't get a scholarship, Papa was earning a lot again, he didn't want to send me anything, and so my dream of medicine ended.

I had to find a job. I was a copyist in an agricultural association, big sacks lay on the floor, the light was always on in the basement rooms, and it was cold everywhere. I ate little and poorly in the cafeteria. Stančić's wife ate every other day then in the same cafeteria, she was still unmarried, she traded off with her sister, they had only enough coupons for one and her hunger was even worse. I had to run away from my second sublet room because the owner of the apartment, an old man, tried to break into my room while his wife was away. That apartment was protected as a cultural monument, people came to see the paintings, those beautiful white Motikas, and I had the room only from six P.M. on, and fear of the old collector.

I found a third sublet room at a doctor's place, his wife drank but that didn't frightenen me so much. I audited classes in archaeology and began working on cartoon films. Often for whole nights. Despite all that was going on the director once said to me, "You work? Why, you look as if you're living off your grandmother's jewelry."

I was lonely, hungry, tired. Two or three married men wanted to get me into bed with them, I couldn't do that. Then I turned twenty-two and got involved fairly soberly with a sober young man, he was a film director, but I didn't keep up the relationship. I was still too romantic. Late sorrows, thoughts about death, publishing the first poems. Free living didn't go entirely well for me, the dark chambers of the body still heard Papa's slaps, that upbringing, that good child. Papa often wrote me letters from Opatija, he philosophized with me. I didn't consider it important at the time that they never sent me a package of food.

Then I met my first husband, a young poet, at the writers' club. He came to our first date with pots full of food. I was touched and in any case ready to escape into a firm relation-ship. We got married in the summer, two well-known writ-ers were the best men, I wore a used dress from the flea mar-ket, we played soccer with an apple in front of the office of the justice of the peace. We didn't especially celebrate that day, those were still the days, back in 1952! Today I often see brides dressed in long white gowns and automobiles decorated with flowers outside that building in Zagreb.

We moved into the one-room apartment with the bath-room-toilet-larder, we translated books from German, he quit his job in the used-book store, typed manuscripts, that's how we lived. Life with Z. was simple at first, he liked to eat plain potatoes and he read a lot. His mother was uneducated and was very meek. On Sundays we would sit in his parents' modest apartment, Z.'s brother lived there too, and I was amazed that they were always silent and read newspapers while they were eating. I tried to start up a stupid, learned conversation but I soon gave it up. That pleased his mother, she would visit me secretly and then would talk like a waterfall, she complained about the silence at home and I composed letters for her to her relatives, she was insatiable when it came to that. Then Z. discovered his love for Africa, we collected wooden sculptures and published books on the poetry of "primitive" peoples. After that it was logically time for surrealism. We sat in the kitchen at Stančić's, or at General S.'s, he was one of the youngest members of the partisan army. He told us stories about the war, about the crimes of the Germans, about the struggle, and then I saw many places in the city with new eyes, my experiences with my own land changed. When Mladen—before the war he had been in prison for twelve years—fell out of favor, we visited him and brought bananas for the children, and after a little while the man who stood outside the house in civilian clothes would greet us like old acquaintances. This was after the Informbureau Resolution, our journal *Krugovi* was attacked, but after a few days we got the money to publish it again. Ervin Šinko spoke against Prévert, whom we wanted to publish, then he said we could publish him anyway. The years were unrestrained and passionate, we had debates every night at the Writers' Union, we read poems in the theater, the salesgirl at the fruit stand had our books, younger people came to see us in our apartment and we had conversations about poetry. We held poetry evenings in villages, we traveled to Bosnia, Macedonia, Dalmatia, I slowly became a part of this country of ours, I was accepted. I forgot about my family, about Opatija, I had a home of my own.

The first almond flowers I saw on the island of Zlarin in 1961 were enormous. I was divorced, I was writing film scripts, we were on location shooting a movie about the islands for Zagreb television. We, that is, the cameraman Tobžić, the actress N., the director Viculin.

From that sunny island, from that garden with trees full of almonds, he had set out long ago, fourteen years old, barefoot, to join the partisans. He drank a lot and told me, "Whenever I go into some bar, all my dead comrades come in with me and then we stand together at the bar, the bars are always full of morning light, we drink to the health of all of us. One glass for you, my dead Marko, one for you Ivica, and for you." Vicko knew the texts I had written by heart, he found the corresponding pictures, we understood each other almost without words, he, the child of the island, and I, daughter of a middle-class family. When depression took control of him we would shoot without him, no one at the television knew anything about it, we kept quiet. Only his tiny, dark-haired wife would sometimes talk with me about his depression, we couldn't find any sort of way out. For seven years I sat with Vicko in village hotels and listened to his stories about the war, about Istria where he was later a traveling actor, about the olive trees of Zlarin. He was a real person and a sufferer.

The young actress was also childlike, pure and uncorrupted. Both of them didn't quite understand the world. Later she would marry a friend and get sick after giving birth. She would give up acting, her career, and sit in her room, silent. I would send her medicines from Germany, because we don't have any in Yugoslavia and all the doctors believe in them. But we couldn't bring her back to reality, she would hang the walls of the room with pictures of her deceased mother, she would remain pretty and slender and would sit with us staring into some strange, foggy distance. We couldn't bring Vicko back to reality either. But that was later. At this time we were still shooting films, we looked in the Bosnian mountains for the partisan hospital where he had typhoid and where they had to amputate both legs of a girl who wanted to become a dancer. "I'll dance with you Vicko, even without legs," she said, then laughed and died. We found the graveyard of that hospital, a green meadow with nameless graves, we lived with peasants in the mountains. There in winter the wolves come right up to the threshold of the house, I wrote by the light of a kerosene lamp, Vicko didn't drink much. In the village school—only seven children went to it, that school by Šator Mountain—we found trunks with rusted surgical instruments and a list of the fallen and the dead. In our film we made that list public and the families of those fighters contacted us, they didn't know where their children were buried, we told them the way to the graveyard in the Bosnian mountains. Later we shot crazier and crazier films, about mirrors, dreams, about autumn. Viculin sang partisan songs on the street at night, he wore very old shoes, he didn't want a bigger apartment, didn't want more money, he longed for the sea. I had to go to the bars with him, he recited Mayakovsky, I would drink two or three brandies, he would drink five, six. I couldn't help him, it was getting harder and harder to shoot films, there were sometimes empty bottles lying in the cutting rooms. One colleague tried to talk with him, Vicko said, "You're all strangers to me, everything is alien, only the dead are real." When I went off to Berlin to the Film and Television Academy he wasn't shooting many pictures anymore, his wife told me that he stayed home, read our old scripts, baked bread every day. He died in the hospital, still young (I came back that summer), he was a comrade to his dead and set out to meet them. True to the end to his friends, family, the sea, and the island of his childhood. Our long-ago films lie forgotten in round tin boxes in the television archives, their titles are completely illegible and no one recognizes them

THE SILK, THE SHEARS

anymore. A graveyard like the one in the Bosnian mountains. I wrote the obituary when nobody knew who he was
anymore.

The Curtains

The inner world of drawers and closets is easier to remember
than the smooth, external form which is too large, which
can't be encompassed, ordered, or taken in hand—while
those numerous details remain clearly before your eyes,
unforgettable. The wardrobe in my parents' bedroom was a
pea-green color, the doors were decorated with red wooden
buttons, the wood inside was pale yellow, gloves of fine
leather lay below, hats, perfumed scarves, the bed linen and
towels were folded on top. Who washed that linen, I don't
know. An old woman washing sheets in a gray laundry room
in an attic full of steam, the soft wrinkled skin of her hands,
was that in Zagreb or was it only a scene remembered from
an old movie?

The table and chairs in the dining room had a shiny, black
finish, the upholstery was green and of rough cloth, you
could push secretly with your fingers under the ornamental
ribbon glued onto its edges, the glue was glassy hard under
your fingers, the hard heads of the nails. In the china cabinet
were blue cups, a porcelain cat, a little gray glass elephant, a
gentle doe of Meissen porcelain. The necks of the wine glasses
were slender, the glasses were bordered with garlands of
more opaque glass, and when they were full they gave off a
silvery glimmer.

The furniture in my sisters' nursery was pink-colored and
huge, ungainly. But a small wicker children's table stood
there too, and two wicker chairs which always creaked softly
when anyone sat on them. The most beautiful of all were the
curtains of rosy tulle at the window. They were covered with

blue and red embroidery, those little garlands were as big as the tips of my fingers and soon were torn here and there. When I stood at the window and put my fingers into those little circles, the tulle in the center of them would tear so easily.

Those curtains were also on that other window in Belgrade, when they dragged me out of bed, I was ten years old, in the middle of the night. Papa was tipsy and still in his tuxedo, Mama with her fat belly in the seventh month was standing in front of the curtains at the window. They had been arguing, he had fallen childishly in love with some secretary at the office, the secretary had given him a brown vase, it's now at Vera's in Homburg. Mama cried, talked about the misfortune and about her condition. Papa shouted, pulled me roughly into the middle of the room and asked whom I would want to stay with in case of a divorce. I know too, for a moment I was sure that I would want to stay with him, but then I couldn't say anything. I felt as if I was torn in two, I was silent and stood trembling in the room in my long nightshirt. Then he hugged me wildly. I pushed his hands away, I was horribly frightened, but at the same time I felt sorry for him, for that sorrow of his and for his seeking consolation in me. The room smelled of wine, they must have both stood there petrified, total silence reigned, and I went slinking back to bed. I dragged that night around with me for years without understanding and full of some kind of fear. We never talked about it, a shadow of sin, a shadow of despair lay over it. Later I talked with my sisters about it, Nada had experienced a similar outpouring of tenderness, she hated Papa because of it, but I think that it was all just unhappiness, loneliness.

In the middle room of the apartment stood the couch I slept on. It was a bed in the shape of a bench with three linen cushions, with bluish yellow embroidered flowers. I got that low couch as a dowry when I got married, it was never wide enough for two and it was pretty rough for us to sleep on it for nine years. Today it's newly upholstered in Mama's room, and when B. and I are in Zagreb we sleep on it again, and again it is cramped. The pictures from our long-ago rooms still hang here too, one from Papa's friend Sirovy who killed himself. It shows a woman seen from behind, her red coat is cut up to the neck, she's walking along some hilly path. For me that woman was always mysterious, without a face, for me she had her eyes closed and was in danger of tumbling into the abyss.

Vera's place in Homburg has the picture of a man looking at the stars, then a drawing of some garden in Vienna, Neuboeck's smoked fish, a big landscape of the Alps and also a picture by Sirovy. The third one is at Nada's.

A silk reproduction of Spitzweg's gardener with cacti, an expensive porcelain owl, the remnants of the dinner service, one blue cup, the little doe which is missing a piece of her head, three plates with red tulips, one thin coffee cup, the little elephant, a glued-together glass box with a parakeet. All these things lie scattered around Mama's room, the pathetic remnants of former spaces. Nothing more was saved, and we too were careless with that old junk, for a long time none of us had any relationship to it. Only our mother sometimes stood unhappily before those remnants of a life. From time to time I think, two more cups, another glass or vase, maybe it would be good if she had them now. The old alarm clock from the night table long ago has a weak and rusty ring, my mother constantly winds it along with two or three other old clocks, but despite that the loss is almost total. And it's as if her memory was swept away with those lost objects.

Elika's Soups

Elika, an aquaintance of my parents, got us out of the shack. She and her daughter also lived on Buconjić Street, we often visited her, she had grown up in Berlin. At that time, during the war, we didn't know that her husband was with the partisans and that she hid members of the underground in her basement as well as all sorts of banned books. She was acquainted with the city's commanding officer and used her German passport to save the lives of many communists. They never found her out, no one informed on her. When the war ended she left her husband and went away to work as a housekeeper in the resort in Opatija where my father would later go. There she met a doctor, soon got married, and returned to Zagreb. When she found out where we were she came to visit with her husband, a black limousine stopped in front of the shack, and he offered my father the job in Opatija. At that time you couldn't get an apartment in Zagreb, Father had to move to new lodgings in any case. Because of school I stayed on at the Šir family's house. I can hardly remember the woman and children, I only recall the room with the piano and that I couldn't go into it until late in the evening.

But I had Elika then and at her house, like everyone who came to see her, I would get a hot lunch and a little bag of cookies for later in the afternoon. For me Elika was the manifestation of a woman who was not like my mother. She would get up at six in the morning, when the first peasants were already arriving, sitting in the corridor or in the kitchen, and she would make hot tea, hearty soup, or coffee for them. I never saw Elika, who shared everything with everyone, cooking, her table was always loaded with the best things as if by a miracle. I never saw her cleaning the apartment, but the beds were always made. She was the first to give me a Brecht-Weil recording to listen to, she kept Käthe Kollwitz's lithograph against hunger in the kitchen, she read completely different books, was involved in politics in the country where she was living. She took me with her to small villages, worked tirelessly for days on end, sang, was lighthearted. And so at Elika's too I sat on a hard kitchen chair and looked closely at life. After work in the cooperative, or after lectures on numismatics or Roman history—one professor read to us from Carlo Levi's book *Christ Stopped at Eboli* the whole semester and only now do I know what a good professor he was—I would run to Elika and she would hug me as no one ever had before.

With time she no longer drew her thin, pencil-traced eyebrows quite as precisely as before. She never forgot the pain her first husband had caused her. Suddenly she was very agitated, she got angry at a lot of unimportant things, disappointment grabbed her by the throat. She was left alone, refused any kind of help, moved into a smaller apartment, began giving German lessons, kept right on cooking good, thick soup for anyone who was poor. Her family was in Germany, she didn't want to leave Yugoslavia, and so today she is still here, running around the city through the cold in sandals, wearing a light old raincoat. Elika cooks, scolds, sings, some people in the city feel that it has all gotten out of hand. She doesn't dye her hair anymore, she helps her friends, she'll soon be eighty, country people still bring her potatoes or cheese, they haven't forgotten her. Her life is just as nimble, full of questions, she persists stubbornly in her own way, fights battles over the price of meat, reads all the newspapers. Now and then she is troubled, disordered in her mind, always radiant. When I visit her today I still sit on a hard chair in her kitchen, I always get a bowl of hot soup, a lecture on socialism, and a kiss when I leave. Elika's hands have gotten rough and calloused, her spirit restless, her heart beats too fast. I'm often afraid for her but she doesn't accept any kind of help at all, I secretly put some small gift under the papers in the kitchen, those gifts of bags of cookies and sugar chime in my recollection. The dark stooped peasants sit in the former hallway, her laugh rings resonantly in the rooms, her arms suddenly hug me, and then every grief is subdued.

So Elika's rough hands have attained their immortality, they remain forever on my face, on my shoulders. They repose there, and as in the old days I walk in my long coat handed down from Aunt Helena in Vienna, at night down Ilica Avenue, I firmly clutch the little bag with the cookies and no longer fear the darkness. I brush against the occasional passerby without restraint and eat the gift of cookies with boys I don't know in the gloomy entryway. I study, I am glad, crouching on the ground with the children, the same as I did long ago.

III

MOVEMENTS

The Operation

In 1954 Z. and I read poems at Kolarac University in Belgrade, we get to know our colleagues there, Popa, Davičo, and eccentric white-haired Ljubiša Jocić. Two days later, on the bus, I get sick on the way back from Novi Sad. My stomach hurts terribly, I keep having to vomit, huddled next to the seat. At five o'clock they take me to a Belgrade hospital. At first the doctors think it is appendicitis, but since the leukocyte count is normal they think it must be something else after all. They keep me in the hospital to continue tests the next day.

I lie alone in the room, the pain gets to be unbearable. I can't stand it anymore and I go out into the corridor in my hospital gown, looking for the doctor's ward. Everything is deserted, silent, dark. The night doctor opens the door when I knock, I manage to tell him, you have to do something now, I can't bear any more, and then I pass out. At ten o'clock I'm lying on the operating table, I don't care what happens to me, just so the pain stops. They give me a local anesthetic and one of the doctors says: Suck in your stomach, relax, breathe, don't breathe. I don't feel the incision on my skin, but after that it's horrible. They take out my appendix after all, I hear that there's a stone in it, it has nearly perforated the wall of the intestine, there was no inflammation, hence the confused symptoms, the low leukocyte count. A doctor with a white mask over his mouth says all this: "Yes, you saved your own life when you came over to our office tonight, an hour later everything would have been much more dangerous. I'll make sure the scar will be small, you'll be able to wear a bikini, young woman."

He later gave me the longish brown stone, for a long time I carried it in my handbag wrapped in a handkerchief, but after a few months it turned into sand.

I wake up the night after the operation, they've put a bag full of sand on the wound in the traditional way, I lie under that weight as if I am strapped down. The pains don't stop, my nose is bleeding heavily, the whole pillow is soaked with blood. I can't find the emergency bell in the room, I agonizingly get hold of my bag on the floor beside the bed and throw it toward the door. I miss. I throw one shoe, then the other. Thud. A young doctor dashes into the room, is alarmed, nervously calls the night nurse. I get a shot to make the blood coagulate. Later he told me it was a good thing that I aimed the shoe so well. The nurse stays in the room the whole night.

The next day Z. comes to visit me with a bag full of oranges and is surprised that I'm so weak, he talks with the doctor. The doctor tells him that I could leave the hospital in three days if I can find someone to stay with in Belgrade and spend three more days in bed. But we don't know anyone in the city.

Two days later, Z. takes me in a taxi to a small house, to Jocić, who had offered immediately to take us in. Jocić lives here with his mother, his ex-wife, a film director, and his young wife Sana. They also have a rabbit, a bird, and there is a sort of marvelous bustle, warmth, and now I'm lying in the middle of that chaotic house. At the time I didn't fully understand their way of living, the freedom taken for granted, that well-being without possessiveness, that absence of the middle-class "I" that Ljubiša propagated. To everyone he was brother, husband, son, and poet. The women lived in harmony, no one was shortchanged in anything, he had a surplus of love, of fairness, a true community ruled in the house. They all spoke openly about their desires, no one lied. He spoke about pictures just as seriously as he did about bed, there was no sort of distinction in importance. Sana was just as happy as the rabbit, the mother, or the film director.

In the evening everyone sat around my bed, writing poems, we talked constantly, didn't sleep very much. Ljubiša took care of me, I forgot about the pain, he told us about Paris where he had lived for a long time and about how the rabbit had furtively eaten up his last novel. There were black curtains in the room, almost no furniture, they gave me the big bed. He didn't have any money, but he brought home the best food from somewhere. He built a doll out of the things in my trunk and christened it in the name of the stone that had brought me to them. He read our coffee grounds for us, Sana wrote us a song, we laughed, we were free, life, joy, tenderness reigned in the room. At our departure we stood at the station with our arms full of his books, his white hair gleamed on the platform for a long time. He was waving to us half an hour after the train had completely disappeared, he told us in a letter.

Young Sana later left him, some other girl had come to stay, but Sana had been wanting to leave anyway. She wanted to go to Paris, she was writing good poems. She wrote to me for a while, today I don't know where she is, she must be back in Belgrade. For a long time Jocić wrote to us in Zagreb, mysteriously and beautifully, once he came to visit us. Later he ran through the streets of Belgrade wearing only a shirt, I never saw him again, I don't know whether he's still alive. Belgrade was too small for him, he was no good at dealing in the literary business, it didn't interest him. But whatever happened, one thing is certain: He lived with a heart that didn't want to possess anything, to take anything for itself—and the middle class called that immorality. Their little house remains in my memory as a place of healing, as a recognizable place of scars that fade. Today I wouldn't be able to find it, the trip there in the taxi was too fast. What has happened to that house, if Ljubiša is no longer there? Do its walls recall that life, or have they made room for new buildings, different people who have no garden, have no animals? And who would never forgive a rabbit for eating up their book.

Father 2

My father's death changed many things. To Mama it seemed like a brief liberation, but a person who has served a long time and struggled in the wrong way can't gain anything truly new from changes. We didn't know that right away, we wanted her to laugh, but she couldn't do it. We rarely visited his grave, Vera planted three cypresses and now their roots threaten to lift the gravestone. To me he left his handwritten reminiscences, a hundred pages in a brown notebook. Forty pages are missing, the ones about his marriage, I don't know where they are. There are few concrete facts in that notebook, it's all more general thoughts about life. I haven't looked at it for years, but even earlier I didn't find the answers to the questions that interested me, tormented me. The love letters to Mama lie in a trunk and are full of basement damp. His traces in us, he wanted to leave more than that—they will disappear with us.

How are things distributed in the family? Vera is just like Father, Nada like Mother, I am half like both of them. I don't know whether that's right. I don't see his vehemence in us, but I see his sicknesses often. The interwoven tensions were not untangled, the contorted stomach remained, fevers swept over us without warning.

His role in that women's story? He always told us that he had wanted only daughters, he wanted to mold them. Coming to terms with a son, I don't know whether that would have been possible. We thought he was handsome and that played a big role, we liked his face, he knew it and never entirely gambled away that admiration.

Papa had his job and the ship that he captained at home. He was certain that only he could do it. Fury at unequal partners, he poured that into our hearts, the opinion that it's not good if only one member of a couple has the right view of things. The wish for all burdens to be carried by two, by three—is that only some kind of utopia, born out of material dependence on him? I have often done too much in that sense. Have I loved to be enslaved because of that long-ago sense of guilt? At one time I felt it was good that he always let us see that it was too much for him, those open beaks at home, those women. But then I was very small, and misunderstandings about guilt are not as fertile as people usually think. We have an urge for giving that is almost pathological.

What happened to his love for Mama? It died, that's what I used to think. Later I learned that loves die without reason, because of time, because of the body. At forty he said that life had passed him by. Did he say that only to us, wanting to be left in peace, not understanding the structure which rests like a burden on the sense organs? Did he know that fidelity was not only possession? And what did we mean to him in that weary life? The hope of possible loves? He criticized all our boyfriends or husbands. I think it was not only jealousy but also self-projection, that groundless sensuality. I never find my father in other men, I don't recognize him, I don't look for him, he didn't leave any residue still in need of discovery. His unmatched power remained, uncurtailed, he was mighty and has remained so. All that's left in me is a lively fear of unrestrained anger; because of that I have always quickly run to gentle people. That lives in the heart and doesn't leave it, because of that I am often obstinate, timid, childish. For he was in some sense a proprietor, he took his place loudly in our dreams, he even managed to make us drag him around with us like a burden, like something severe and inexplicable. Because of that we didn't mature at home, he sent us off his boat as naive girls, our steps were blocked, we were stupid and sure of everything. We had to pay tribute to that papa in us, we had to carry him with us like a climbing vine of death, ask it all the questions and justify ourselves to it, when we stood before others in the various rooms of life. Does that insight mean somewhat more freedom or is it just one path that we run along, here, in these shoes of ours? I think a person can take off the shoes when she no longer feels pity and no longer asks questions of guilt.

I grasped that his early death lent truth to his life after all. The stern look changed, I understood his vehemence because of the brevity of life. When I see us like that at home around the table, when I see how he saw us—he came home from work, hanging his hat on the hook rather wearily—perhaps then I would throw all the cups off the table too, maybe I too would howl helplessly, demanding the unity of all evil worlds. I don't know for sure, children see their parents wrongly and rightly. Only fear and the urge for death sharpen our eyes, allow us to experience the true significance and then pour a rosiness or a pallor over us.

So I ask questions and don't receive answers either from him or from Mama. When it was still possible he would shout nervously and I was too stupid. Now we have to be satisfied with nothing but the climbing vine.

In his love letters to Mama he was still a young man with a light step, he smiled carefully, life, all possibilities were ahead of him. That's how I hold him in memory, I can still do that, and I can direct his steps into the street where he wanted to go. He nods his head to me, lifts his hat, and leaves forever.

A Man of Ice

Marriage with Z. had many outlines. The literary one was the least distorted. Yesenin and the freedom to recite poems anywhere, that was in fashion then. Z. was married to a musician before I knew him. He was expelled from the university because he came to lectures in an Eden hat and because he spoke against Zhdanov. My resistance to that hat was immense, and we buried that hat together. He went around without it and without a cap, shaved off his mustache, believed in automatic writing. Only art interested him, only dreams. I wanted to talk with people, I would spend hours with our neighbor, who told me about her childhood in Macedonia, where before the war girls would marry the man who was satisfied with their dowry. And since she was poor, she had been married to a tailor who had a shop in Zagreb. Her husband was so stingy that he gave her no money at all, he even shopped for the food. She sat at home and cooked, gave me ten dinars to keep for her, and even then ten dinars was nothing. Z. never knew what to say with her, he was quiet in general and didn't care for those trivial interests of mine. We often sat in the Writers' Club and after a certain time he didn't talk there anymore either, he started to play solitaire. In the beginning I was a good kibitzer, later I would play along with him, but before long it all started to bore me.

Z. was actually emotionally stingy. I liked that after all the ferocious scenes at home. I didn't believe in the various tales my father passed on to me by way of a professor in Zagreb, and so our marriage was infantile, tenderness was infrequent, but I was only a little girl myself. I started to betray Z.

platonically. It was always writers I fell in love with in my thoughts, faulty upbringing took its revenge. The soul, not really knowing what it is, took the first place in everything. I was living almost ethereally then, and I thought that if I left—once I even tried to, but I came back from the station and got a lovely yellow scarf—then he would die of starvation or sorrow. We lived on translations, I took dictation on the typewriter, he was upset that I was too slow. Naturally I didn't learn to walk around the house naked, I didn't know how to summon up that earthy excitement, before long I didn't even think about it anymore. I reconciled myself to everything, I was afraid I might hurt his feelings, I kept silent. Appeased my hunger with infatuations. It was the life of a little girl, just false crutches.

In Rovinj, where we had a fisherman's cottage, I would meet—leaving the house on tiptoe—with a certain well-known and married writer in the woods at the crack of dawn, and we would kiss as fiercely as if we were nineteen years old. A couple more wrote me letters, we played the game of truth by Saint Euphemius's Church in the evening. Z. wasn't a favorite with people, the years went by. I wasn't unhappy with him, we spent a lot of time with other people, we no longer talked about essential things.

I betrayed Z., as he did me, after eight years, in a small room with the blinds drawn, with a bad conscience and a poorly chosen man. It was one of those sons who keep track of how many women they've slept with, but that wasn't the worst part. The next day I happened to find out the sleazy way he was advancing his theatrical career, and how he was in fact the epitome of an informer. I was perplexed, I didn't understand how it was possible for me to suspect nothing of the kind, and, just as I was going to resign myself to self-denial all over again, I noticed—I had already been working on the television for six months because you couldn't live off translations anymore—that Nada and her girlfriend were avoiding me, and that perhaps washing laundry was not the only thing going on in the apartment before noon.

It was one afternoon, I can still see myself now sitting on our low couch while Z. stood before me at the balcony door and looked out into the yard. He never did that. By some inspiration I asked him, "You're in love with another woman, aren't you?" He slowly turned around, it was just like in some movie, and answered softly, "Yes." In spite of everything, that struck me terribly. I had believed that this mutual literary life of ours was eternal. I thought of the years that had passed, of everything that I had done, that I hadn't done, and one stupid tear ran down my cheek. He, naturally, interpreted that tear to his own advantage and immediately took pains to tell the whole truth. He wanted only three months of freedom for this passion that was new to him as well. He knew the span of time exactly, only that much, I should understand, after that it would all be over and we would go on living as before. She was just a forbidden fruit that interested him, that girl who was like a little wild animal, yes, that's the way he said it. She was also an unhappy creature, maybe he should go away with her somewhere, maybe to Paris, and so forth. I listened to what he was saying and at the same time I thought, catching the second tear above my mouth with the tip of my tongue, if this is the case, then it's also a chance to escape, grab it. I thought too, insulting myself, that naturally no one wants to kill a fat goose while it's laying. That would be stupid, for a trip to Paris you need money as well. I only said, "All right," painfully, like in some bad play, "go." He stopped talking, he was sad, I said nothing. And so, nothing else was possible, he left the apartment. Without any of his things, just in his shirt and trousers.

I went on sitting alone in the room, I was still thinking about where he had gone to now. Then our neighbor came in, she had heard him leave and started telling me all sorts of incoherent things right away. I just wanted to be alone, I wanted to think everything over, and for a short time I was vain enough to understand nothing and thought of everything as a great loss. But that story later took on even more colors. Z. waited for me every day in front of the television station, he had gotten noticeably thinner, he didn't want to lose me completely. Nada broke all ties with her friend, her friend sent word that Nada should stop thinking badly of her, because she was in love too. Mama said, "Everything will blow over, there's no point in a divorce, all this is just a little slip after eight years, it's nothing, that girl is lying." Stančić said, "Stay on your own, that's good, think everything over." Viculin was a real friend, I told him everything one sunny morning in the yard on Šubić Street, standing by the warm brick wall. He didn't leave me on my own, he asked the television to give us a car so we could leave for Istria even though the screenplay wasn't finished yet. Of course the young assistant director fell in love with me right away, the coast was clear now, he climbed onto my balcony at night, gave me Hesse's *Steppenwolf*, Vicko finally got him calmed down. The phone in the apartment rang constantly. My friends, except for wise Angelo, condemned Z. The circle closed, I could no longer breathe in Zagreb, we left for filming in Istria and I became allergic to the sun for the first time.

I was sorry, Nada and I cried, we couldn't talk in private. I had no faith in a future with Z., everything was confused, we were helpless. Overly injured, I made mistakes, everything was mistaken. Those mixed feelings went on for two months and then I was free. The air went clear again. Z. wrote me that he wanted to live with me and that was true, he didn't get married again. He stayed with Nada's friend for a long time. At that time some tall blond would cook lunch in his apartment at noon. Then he split up with Nada's friend. I started talking with her, she also worked in television. She later got married and later on divorced. She was a very good worker, but there was a scandal because of an anti-Semitic declaration aimed at her. We composed the text for the workers' council meeting together, people didn't understand us anymore. It was hard for her then in our small city, I told Z. that, she had drawn all the hatred onto herself. With us it's the women who are always blamed for everything. After her divorce I really came to love her, but all that no longer did her much good. She had a biting sense of humor, I liked her more and more, we talked too about the child she wanted so much. Like me, she didn't dare to have a child alone and without a husband. We hadn't succeeded in casting off the chains of society, it was a long time ago. Now she's back living with her mother and listening as I once did to that same old litany: "You've ruined your own life, you have only yourself to blame for everything."

In the meantime Z. has gained a little weight, perhaps he has a blond girlfriend again, he writes poems, publishes a lot of books and translations. I don't know whether he still takes photographs. He is a grandfather, the daughter from his first marriage had a child. I don't know much more than that about him. He has a cat and a turtle at home, maybe he's lonely. When I meet him these days, it seems to me that I'm meeting a stranger, I no longer remember that we lived together. His quietness doesn't bother me, but I don't know whether we would understand each other now. We no longer know anything about each other. And so when we meet we drink coffee, he gives us his new books, we talk about poetry. Furthermore, he wants to help me in everything, I ask how his eyes are, and that's all. When I go to shake his hand I don't look him in the face, when he kisses me good-bye no warmth passes through our bodies. I sense that it's too bad for me too. But that ice no longer melts. Both of us have failed to change that. We buried a mutual life which did have tenderness in a snow which no longer thaws. The familiar winter comes over me and, as usual, I only now cast my ridiculous youth off my shoulders.

Questions

What was our women's life like in Zagreb? I see women with heavy handbags in the street, I see them laughing and smoking in cafés, I see grandmothers with their grandchildren in the parks, the daughters are at the office or the factory. I see little Mrs. K. in her eternal dressing gown who came to the city from the poor karst regions, came to the basement apartment in our building and said to everyone, "Ah, you poor soul!" I see the faces of the girls who were tortured in prisons in the war, the face of Nada S. with shrapnel under her scalp. I see this city, the blue streetcars, the acquaintance who hanged herself in the basement under the room where we once sat together. I got to know her before she lost so much weight, that summer at the beach where she was swimming with her daughters. She told us stories, laughing, about her crazy father who thought he was made of glass and that he would break. But then her older daughter got sick, she was depressed and then she got sick too and couldn't bear it any longer. I think of Dora, whom I worked with on theater broadcasts for the television in the summer in Dubrovnik. At night we perched on the bed and laughed at the theater's main Don Juan, who thought everyone was in love with him. Now she rarely leaves her apartment, is afraid of the dark, cold stairway, is afraid of the street, eats hardly anything, works a lot, doesn't know what it all means. We have to take care of her, her skin is very pale from the air in her room.

Is this the end of a class in our country, the rift which is growing obvious, while newcomers and new residents of the city arrive in its place? They set up their apartments, buy automobiles, work in Germany, build weekend cottages, buy bathroom tiles in Trieste the same way I used to buy pretty shoes, believing that the ones there were the prettiest. Is this the crucial turning point when little girls perish, the playful companions of my childhood? Or do women sense more clearly than men that we are only patching together the old forms? Are women differently helpless because they're differently alone, since they only cook and have children? And so there's not enough time for thinking things over? So we don't have time for conversations, descriptions of the situation, we don't catch up with the changes while the new city people are already catching our diseases? The Pill, the diaphragm, abortion—accepted without question; makeup, powder, irresistible beauty—accepted without resistance? Is it only fear of old age that's left in the rooms in the end, tormenting and stretching the withered skin, the fatal betrayal?

I'm not always in Zagreb either, and for my friends I have ventured into the glittering kingdom of a horizon of department stores. No one would believe me if I said it wasn't so. The experiences of local, of Western destruction don't tend to be easily noticed, because it's only a matter of individuals. With them or without them—in that way any possible solidarity is destroyed. And so what remains in the end is often the hook we hang ourselves on. I couldn't say that to my acquaintance, I didn't see her again. But even if I could have, it wouldn't have done any good, I wouldn't have changed anything. It was too late. So we must find other ways of comfort, contact, and strength. The pattern of connections in life is not in good enough condition to endure.

A certain actress was ready to run off with a Frenchman, and where to? This talented woman was going to work in a shop in Dijon, because she could no longer hold out after two unhappy marriages on her own in a beautiful garret on the far side of the Sava River. Does it always have to be that way once maturity overtakes us, when prospects become clear, when satisfaction in mere objects no longer functions? Fortunately she couldn't do it after all. But in spite of that she thinks she always has to be beautiful, she has to dye her hair, she has to be liked, and by the directors as well, otherwise she won't get any more good parts. Does she only think so or is that really the way things are? Things really are that way. So then must she say to hell with her vocation? And then the shop in Dijon after all. It looks as if it's too late for everything. As a child she was forbidden to laugh loudly, and now she laughs onstage when she can. Over time her parts have gotten smaller and smaller, she stands alone in her kitchen, desolation climbs up the walls. Did that old-style upbringing of ours bring us only to fear?

I went away by chance and without intending it to be for long. I wasn't holding the steering wheel in my hands either, probably I was looking for a stupid kind of happiness. As it looks today, that is what I would like to see in the rearview mirror of the car that drives only to old age. I wouldn't want us to remain sitting in rooms, beneath pictures and hanging lamps, surrounded by old letters and with false lashes on our eyes.

Ankica, a country girl from Metković, played at home with pebbles instead of dolls. Now she works in Berlin as a house-cleaner, also cleans the staircase of the building she lives in, cleans her apartment, polishes the furniture, wipes away the dust. Where does that pressure come from, who crammed all that into her head? Does the stale air from the rooms of our childhood penetrate everywhere? Are the old standards of our parents deathless? Cleanliness, tidiness, order. In the evening she sits wearily with her husband in front of the television, they don't talk. So life goes by. Why always only new things, new words and clothes? Always sweeping every tiny crumb from the table—anything else might mean that they don't know the meaning of cleanliness, or order. The desire not to possess an expensive tea service or expensive curtains on the windows, that desire isn't contagious at all. A child doesn't have to have only good grades, fashionable glasses, doesn't have to become a German child—to her those facts aren't important. I tell her, "Drop all that, live." But that's impossible when it's a matter of insecure people, and not only their life is in question, but ours too, that of our parents and their ideals.

On the gray streets a child stands, and the parents hold it firmly by the hands. It learns to talk, to walk, to read. It repeats what they tell it. It repeats too, so easily, the life of grown-up, superior people. Sometimes it doesn't know of anything that isn't prechewed or artificially colored. I look on that street for what lies behind us, I look into the past and pull myself out of it. Or at least I hope so.

The City

The city has lived, it has had to, with its fear of the next earthquake, with eternally overcrowded streets, with peeling facades. It isn't modest like Berlin, its windows are open, without velvety curtains. They show dressers with trunks on them or with bottles of cherries ripening in rum, unmade beds, chairs with clothes hanging over the back, a table with coffee, newspapers, an open wallet. Loud laughter or crying penetrate outside. And all the basement apartments are full of children, women, men. I always think of the poisonous fumes of the roadways, which don't rise upward. The light of the city is warmly yellow, smoky, the factories are close by, and the sky often looks as if a storm is about to break.

Beautiful, strong girls walk elastically across the squares, their eyes are large and made-up, high school graduation is still celebrated with loud whistles, the epidemic of listlessness hasn't broken out here yet. The benches around the old parks are full of pairs of lovers. Many young soldiers sit here, or in the sweetshops, peasant men and women sleep near the main train station, their baskets are neatly lined up alongside the benches, people sit on them and read the newspapers, kiss each other, eat sandwiches, ask me whether I have a light and what time it is.

Laundry drips from the balconies, the heavy washing of overfull apartments, the inhabitants of the city walk along the sidewalks and along the streets, between the streetcars that ring or the cars that honk. It's as if all the seams of the city are bursting.

An old man wearing only a thin raincoat over his naked body hugs me in a bar, he's not afraid of the cloth of my coat and says, "Come back, child." He heard us speaking German. A woman on Ilica Avenue kisses us and wishes us a happy Easter, a drunk at the train station won't take money for carrying our suitcases, he wants to chat with us. All those friendly affable people still live in the city, the country people haven't been driven out as they have been in Berlin, the southern highways only slowly find their place between concrete and soft earth. Embankments with tracks bring soot and smoke, white steam rises above the platform, above the bushes with the red lilies, the kiosks with newspapers, above the people, the multitude of a long wait. When rain falls, it pours all at once, punctured rain gutters flood the sidewalks, people curse the weather, or love, or from time to time the slow pace of socialism. The umbrellas are black and large, everyone willingly bets with a handshake, everyone gets excited easily, someone whistles after every woman. The city dogs are different from the dogs in Berlin—they don't bark, they aren't aggressive, they just want us to pet them. In the shops sugar is sometimes sold in paper bags, next door to the most modern self-service supermarkets, you can still touch the fruit with your hands, people still carry on conversations with the salesgirls about their husbands and children. When you come in again, they recognize you, they greet you like an old acquaintance, they still remember faces.

Both gradual and quick changes keep people awake. There is an old man who always sits on a bench in the park at the same time, at noon a woman selling violets always stands like a statue on the same corner in Gajeva Street, you hear someone practicing the piano at eleven o'clock in Mesnička Street. The waiter at the Gradska Café, a bank teller, the peasant woman with the best cheese, all of them recognize you even after many years. The jasmine bushes and linden trees grow unbelievably fast, the roses in the gardens are enormous and aren't planted in strict rows, there are still glass balls in those gardens as Stančić's pictures show them. Ivy climbs up the walls, its luxuriance, the luxuriance of the hedges isn't trimmed. The same policewoman has stood at our crossing for several summer seasons and if I'm polite I never have to pay a fine for jaywalking. Certainly, those people who live with fear of an earthquake sometimes want different novelties or luxury. Here and there you already see the first Mercedes or Citroën, the first rudeness, the anonymity of the supermarkets, brusqueness, meat with estrogen. We're being overtaken by the measure of a world that despises gray facades, slowness, the smell of sweat, and anyone who's afraid of that has a hard time getting out of the way.

But what is derisively called "Balkanism" in the West, what they seem to dislike but really long for, that still exists a little. Chaos, liveliness, that other brotherhood, and I wish a long duration to all of it. It doesn't matter to me if some call it a weakness, an effect of history or of nature. You can't have everything, the peasant cities will be lost in the distant future, perhaps even without an earthquake. Perhaps people will abandon them because it's easy to get your shoes dirty in them, because now and then storms rain down, because the streetcar doesn't come for a long time. And because it appears that that's the only important thing. Yes, to many people it's the only important thing. I have often felt that way too. The consolation of being a migrant came to me too late, I know as well that to say it that way doesn't always do any good. But now a lot of things have changed, I am getting sick of that other, cold beauty of order, and I'm prepared to wait for hours in the rain for the last streetcar. In the place that stays that way, so "awful" in that way, there we're at home, and I'd like to be only there.

An Unrestrained Person

Stančić was six-and-a-half-feet tall and weighed 325 pounds. He always wore several sweaters, a hat on his head even indoors, and he wore ragged pants and shoes even after he had bought a house.

He told me, "The strength it took to get from a little room in Varaždin to Zagreb, now and then I don't have that strength for the pictures." He knew about the unattainable advantages of the middle classes, the advantage when you're dealing with art, dealing with the market for art. I could have said the opposite: the strength it took to learn what reality was, a voluntary jump off the safety net of those advantages, was not always enough for me to be believed. I abandoned the friends of my middle-class childhood and learned that they'll often push you back into your own nest: No, don't fly, crying won't do you any good. I often had to live in the light of a room, my longing for the air and sun remained unsatisfied for a long time. Unsearched horizons, brotherhood with those peasants by Šator Mountain seemed impossible. I was and remained guilty and that impelled me toward an equation: pains and pondering.

Stančić too in the beginning was ready to think that I despised his clothes, his ancestry, the hard childhood. Long ago in Varaždin he had known only children who didn't want to play with him because of those things. He punished me with reproaches for a past of ignorance, he used to say, "No, it can't be that you're sitting with us, and not with the others, better ones, your own kind."

When I got divorced he said (it was in the evening, we were walking along Zrinjevac, on the left side because of the superstition that the right side brings misfortune), "When the light's on at home I never turn it off, because then the house would be lost. I never walk on the right side of the park, but in spite of that I'll die soon, at fifty, like you too, with your eyes from the oval pictures on gravestones. I worry about my wife and child, we could all have loved one another, nothingness will catch us all quickly. You're crazy, your father is crazy, once when he visited me, I was in the middle of drying a canvas on the floor, he thought it was a white carpet and walked across the painting canvas, the white surface was covered with the prints of his shoes. Your husband wasn't for you, he was too introverted, we're all lost. I'm going to paint another completely black picture, it won't be a tired picture the way you fear, help me."

I knew that in his life there had long ago been infatuations, the daydreams of youth last a long time, but I didn't want to lose our life as a foursome, as a threesome, I loved his wife Melita, I loved him: Everything that could have happened, I didn't know how to act about it. I wanted to maintain that reality, those conversations, and suddenly I also knew—I was ashamed, his body frightened me, while his spirit or soul were like a brother's to me, unique. I said it that way. Or was it again the love of a thirteen-year-old girl that I wanted to hold onto, that projection into time which never has a body? Stančić was sure of that. He didn't offer a favor, he did it otherwise, he believed that everything has its price. And I, I was like Slavenka, I believed in souls touching. And so we all loved each other in different ways, by day each lived in his own world, in the evening we sat together, talked about everything, about hate, about desires, it was a passionate discussion with no end. We were bound by chains which gave us power for those twenty-five years together, the time until distance or death separated us.

With him it was almost impossible to have other friends, he ruled over us. It was also a kind of revenge and only my leftovers remained, that's too little for others. He was constantly on guard, he found some flaw in every woman, every man, he talked about that while I sat in the studio, he painted. More and more often Melita searched for her own peace, we were often exhausted by his monomania, hated the brutal outbursts and the way the rhythm of his life threatened her painting more and more. She became quiet and somewhat dreamy. His enormous body pushed us aside, his daily routine was the law, only that way could new pictures be created, the money to live. Sleeping, talk, painting. Guests in the evening. Melita would disappear into the kitchen, she cooked fabulously, took care of all of us, and in the end believed herself that her talent wasn't all that important. Now and then I would beg her to paint but she didn't want to. Maybe it was impossible next to such a wild, unrestrained man?

I had already noticed long before that in our society sons married meek wives, vegetable wives. The others, the ones who ask a lot of questions, are good as neurotic mistresses, but a person doesn't want to be burdened with them every day. At best one theoretically does something for one's "intelligence" and thinks: It's good if they finally change, if they finally get free. I saw that and my fury was great. So does it all come down to making peace, to giving up the desire for symmetry, to practicing womanly submissiveness? Does a person become lonely if he or she asks for too much?

Melita knew about those questions of mine, but she was truly gentle. And so there was a home, there were quarrels. My role was to make peace from time to time, he loved her beautiful lips, she didn't believe all the stories. Meek women, meek friends, the ones who have to be that way so as not to remain mere guests in life. I would like to talk with them, but the criticism that I'm unaccountable comes at once to the lips, life is difficult enough without that, and then home is a place with a bed to sleep on. My mother knew that, we all knew that sleeping could be deadly, but in spite of that the real conversations are often carried on outside the house. There we experience the strong and transient loves while we live with those others, with the vegetables who don't ask a lot and whom we believe in differently, in whom we find the meaning of the passing days differently. And later the waves can no longer be calmed, the pictures change, people seek consolation in objects.

In the evening guests, artists, friends. Different times. A television set in the room, different conversations. It seemed to Miljenko that all the wounds would finally heal under a new light eiderdown comforter. Now we often quarreled with icy words, the torn clothes were the symbol of former scorn. But when I wanted to leave he was unexpectedly the same as long ago, he spoke differently, hope never deserted the three of us. He possessed the intuition of a prophet, the merciless eyes of the Varaždin townspeople of long ago who had given him a wakefulness which always came to the surface anew. That always restrained me, he substituted for the unlived days of my childhood, taught me to hate, to shout, to laugh: The wiltedness of my still-incomplete escape into another world filled with signs of life. He was simultaneously kind and stern, the old norms of upbringing no longer applied. I was glad that life didn't have to be only pretty or ugly, he never lied.

With time his body grew heavy, he no longer left the house much, he would say that he had no legs. Around two o'clock in the morning we all had to get into the car and Melita would drive us cautiously—she was nearsighted—through the deserted city. He longed so much for those drives that he could be blackmailed, he could be punished by not being driven, and then he would beg, "Drive me, please drive me, Melita."

I see us sailing through those nights toward the intersection with the highway, aimlessly, toward the last streetcar stop or above the hill, with the city lights below us. He sang loudly and uninterruptedly in the car, we would risk our necks. Melita didn't like driving, but it had to continue, that nightly drive. It was a desire for movement, a desire for what he no longer knew, a small substitute for moving forward.

But when he painted *New Zagreb* I found in that picture all those nights united in one, their diffuse light, and suddenly I knew that he always returned to the suburbs, to the edge of the shining. He sang the songs of vagabonds, the songs of transients in the car. He would say, "My room is an ice cube, the lines on the pictures are only the symptoms of local diseases. I can't go to Paris as a painter should, I don't want to start down that road, it's too distant, my scale is the provincial one and always will be, the yellow light, they can all just. . . ."

At home he had all the books from museums he couldn't visit, there wasn't a bed in any hotel to suit him. He had seen the sea only once, as a child. He was excited, it was snowing when they arrived, so his father got into the first train back with him, and so that never came to anything either. He was afraid of cholera, the plague, fish bones in his throat. Later on he no longer wanted to paint the pictures that everyone desired, he penetrated more and more into the essence of coercion, he quarreled with half the city, bought wine and food for his students at the Academy, had a thousand phobias. In the summer an electric stove burned in the room, and then he found a doctor who would treat him at home, his bed in the hospital was empty. A doctor who didn't torment him when the time to leave came and, when they took him to the hospital, who sat for hours next to him, held his hand, cried, and after his death wrote a long poem.

Since he is no longer alive our homeland has changed, a big part of my life left with him, the fat child of the pictures has vanished beyond return and is silent. Melita put a white cover on his bed in the room, an unfamiliar, new color, we just looked at each other and were silent too. She has remained gentle and meek, she has started painting. She wants to give me some of his personal things, she still hasn't gotten around to it.

He died, he was fifty-one years old, one Friday the thirteenth. His sister from Varaždin wrote that she speaks with him every night.

Movement

Suddenly I got tired in Zagreb. After fifty-some screenplays—the monthly average was one—I couldn't keep on writing anymore, I felt as if I was in a rut. I was writing them too easily. The dream of the everyday began, everything flowed smoothly, the time of postwar poverty had passed. Loves quickly went by, I took a taxi even to the television studio, which wasn't far from my apartment. I no longer had the wish to jump into Stančić's big shoes—he called them children's coffins—and to make him laugh while Melita brought in a nice cake and we sat in the living room. Viculin was away on a trip into darkness. The television, money, those were the themes.

I had met Erich Kubi in 1951 at an exhibit. He wanted to find something out, I translated it for him, and we soon concluded that I would be the translator of his books. And so I was. Then he told me how in January of 1943 he had escaped ahead of Hitler on a bicycle into Yugoslavia. His girlfriend found a job in Zagreb, he lived off his savings in a little room in Samobor and painted. But soon he had no more money, the relationship with his girlfriend became complicated, he went away to Split, there he ate only bread and figs, once he sold a picture to some Americans and bought a small, deserted island. He had plans for political work abroad. But he didn't know the language and soon realized that he could only have a political effect in Germany, and so in December he left Split, with no money, that possessor of a small island. We wrote to each other from 1951 on and saw each other again after many years. I was already divorced, he had come to Zagreb to attend the congress in opposition to the atom bomb. Erich was the first to say to me, "It would be good if for once you saw the life you lead from a distance, from somewhere else." He sent me application forms for the Film and Television Academy in Berlin. I got an unpaid leave from Zagreb television, I set out, looked for a cheap student's room in Berlin. The upbringing from coddling to abandonment had come to an end, that childhood, the ruined marriage. I cut the umbilical cord, I was thirty-six years old. The dust fell on the empty room in Bulić Street, the neighbor no longer knocked on the door, the pictures and books gradually turned gray. I left with one trunk and found myself somewhere else, for the first time I was completely alone. The friends who stood at the airport waved to me morosely and without understanding.

But I was mistaken too, I didn't find the distance I was looking for, I was frightened in a strange place. And if I hadn't found Benno and the possibility of work together, what would have happened then? In the cold and unfriendly cor-

THE SILK, THE SHEARS

ridors of the Academy I would not have lasted for more than a year. When I greeted people in the morning, everyone laughed at me; when I didn't greet them, no one noticed me. Not even the secretary Helena, the only *person* there, could prevent that. The gloom of the city would soon have frightened me, the difficult loneliness of the people, the grumpy women in the stores, the dog's heart of the streets, the cemented future, that slow ice. I would have quickly gone back to the old nest and there I would have aged. For Vicko would have come to his end, Stančić would not have been spared his sickness, I would have told Mama which dress to put on, what to cook, and nothing would have changed. I would have kept on working on the television, I would have written poems, perhaps I would have married Z. again. Everything would have been the same as long ago. We would have waited for old age, he would have met me in the evening outside the television building with the car, shielded me from small adventures, perhaps he would not have gained weight, and that would be all. Stella would not have been resurrected, the actress from our Zlarin filming would have remained in her room, my friend from Dubrovnik too. I would have chatted with Nada about the invincibility of everyday life, I would have written my sister Vera letters to the desert of Homburg. The strong trap of aging would have seized me. There would have been no movement, that zero point, new pain, the cut through the old silk of childhood. The people here, in Berlin, would not have existed, nor this text, this recollection. In my old life I would have visited my graves and prepared one for myself.

Did I move through some alien land in search of my own land, did I condemn myself because of that to halt in a spaceless Between? Or would I have awakened there as here after many years, so as to see the pattern of the little sea-horse, the dull shears and that old shop?

The microscope moves everything closer, steps across distances, that battle for time. Language is the homeland where we stand, and bread is its noon. The blood between different languages, it lies on my heart, it sets me free, and my legs run with all the bows, dolls, climbing vines. Is the utopia of true understanding despite geographic distance only a passion or only error? Ah, my heart is still too terrified, my skin ages quickly, the pencil scratches, wounds the paper, while memory once again experiences all the prayers and sins and is better than I am. Reluctance, patience. We are moving.

Page from a Diary

Suzana, she is studying medicine, asks: Do you suffer that way too when your friends desert you? She stands with her guitar at the Steglitz subway station and feels in her stomach the same anger that I felt long ago.

At the same station five days ago some young man hit a drunk for no reason, hit him in the face with a newspaper, and then went away without saying a word. That was at six o'clock in the morning, we were coming back from the kitchen in Rothenburg Street, and this time it was ruled by darkness and cold.

Karolina Müller, owner of a gallery, gave me a book about the Mexican painter Frida Kahlo and I lost heart, because I realized that I never could have painted, that bed of suffering where she lay sick for years on end, I wouldn't have had such a strong desire for life. The little strength which we possess is undercut like a bush. In that I understand Suzana's mother well, while the empty Berlin railway carries a few friends to the Eastern sea, into the December wind if there is any. They all want to feel something, to tremble from the cold, maybe to freeze.

Claudio once said, "Villages die in diaries too." Ivan, a worker from Yugoslavia who lives here, said yesterday, "I've been in Berlin for ten years, my child won't have any idea of the difference between home and abroad, perhaps he will lose both concepts in the name of the economy that they sell us here as the meaning of life."

The continuity of relationships constantly breaks up, life shatters them and cools us down. Is that why Vicko searched for his comrades? Have I seen childhood, youth, only because they're past? Is the menacing ahistoricity of the present age that foreign place which takes us by surprise everywhere? The cold embrace of time which allows only sketches of the contours of the hanged or the dead? Only our own biography stops at that point where it catches us. Opens our eyes.

Along Šator Mountain in Bosnia the primroses will soon burst into bloom. The snow will thaw. Far from there, I note down that the apartment is cold, that the telephone doesn't ring. I see the date on the calendar and forget it. A motorcycle drives through the deserted, holiday streets of Berlin, through my head, drives endlessly. I make a note for tomorrow: Buy oil, bread, write a letter to the lawyer for Vinka's residence permit, read, talk with B. Write. In spite of the noises in my head.

■ □ ■ □ ■

MARINA; OR,
ABOUT BIOGRAPHY

Translated by Celia Hawkesworth

■ □ ■ □ ■

New Year Letter

Happy New—light, world, realm, haven—to you,
My first epistle to you in your new
—To call it lush would be miscomprehension—
Lush, ruminant place: clamorous, stentorian
Like the deserted tower of Aeolus.
My first epistle to you from yesterday's
—In which, without you I shall fret and pine—
Homeland, already now, for you, from one
Of heaven's stars . . . Law of retreat, withdrawal,
By which any woman is left by anyone at all,
And unreal ones by unrealities.
Shall I tell you how I learned of yours?
There was no earthquake, no abyss's yawn.
Someone walked in—not loved, just anyone.
"It's an event that's causing great distress.
In *News* and *Days.* I hope you'll do a piece?"
"Where?" "In the mountains?" (Window, fronds of firs,
A bedsheet.) "Don't you read the newspapers?
You'll do one then?" "No." "But . . ." I make excuses.
Aloud: "Too hard." Inside: "I'm not a Judas."
"In a sanatorium." (A rented paradise.)
"When?" "One, two days ago. My memory's not precise."
"Will you talk in Alcazar?" "No, I think not."
Aloud: "His family." Inside:" All but Iscariot."

Happy break of day! (Tomorrow you were born!)
Shall I tell you what I did after I learned . . . ?
Sh. Out of habit my tongue slips and stammers,

I've long since set both life and death in commas,
As being known-to-be empty gossip, false.
I did nothing. But then something else,
Something that does with no echo and no shade,
Was done . . .

           Tell then, how was the trip you made?
How was it that the heart tore, yet was not torn
Apart? As if on Orlov trotters borne,
They that have an eagle's speed, *you said,*
Taking breath away? Or else perhaps it sped
More, and more sweetly? There exist no heights,
Descents for anyone who has known flight
On real Russian eagles. We are blood-related
With the beyond. Who's been to Russia's sighted
The next world in this one. Well-oiled transition!
I smile a hidden smirk in the pronunciation
Of "life" and "death"—my smile's touched by your own.
I say "life," "death" with footnotes added on,
An asterisk (the night I wish were near:
Instead of a cerebral hemisphere—
A stellar one!)

           My friend, do not forget
The following: if the Russian alphabet
Has pushed the German characters away
It's not because now all's one, as they say,
And dead men (beggars) swallow anything,
Don't bat an eyelid!—But because it's plain
—Thirteen, in Novodevichiy, this dawned—
The *next* world isn't tongueless, but all-tongued.

Not without sadness now I ask, implore:
Don't you want to know the Russian for
Nest? The only rhyme for all nests (*gnyozdy*)
Is one that covers all of them: (*zvyozdy*).

Did I stray from the point?

                              That can't be true.

There's no such thing as one that strays from you.
Du Lieber, every syllable and thought
Leads back to you again, no matter what
The theme (though German's really more my own
Than Russian, Angel-talk's most mine). In the same way
As there's no place you aren't—there is: the grave.
All as it wasn't, as it was—but have
You nothing anywhere about me there?
Your surroundings, Rainer, what your feelings are?
Most urgently, and with an assured force,
Your first impression of the universe
(i.e. impression from the poet in it)
And last vision of our earthly planet,
That's given but once to you—and as a whole!
Vision not of ashes-poet, body-soul
(To isolate one's to offend them both)
But of you with yourself, of you betrothed
With you—being Zeusian doesn't mean one's better—
In you each Pollux meets up with his Castor,
In you each marble statue meets its grass,
Not separation, not a meeting—this,
A confrontation: a meeting and
First parting.

                    How did you look at your hand
(and at the trace made on it by the ink)
From all your many (how many, do you think?)
Miles—infinite because beginningless—
Height up above the crystal levelness
Of the Mediterranean—and other saucers.
All as it wasn't, will be, with me also
Placed far beyond the suburbs' outer spheres.
All as it wasn't, all as it appears

—What's that to someone writing letters one
Week extra? And where else should one's eyes turn
As one leans on the theater loge's edge,
From this—except to that, and from that stage
Except to the longsuffering *this:* all views look down.
I live in Bellevue. It's a little town
Of nests and branches. Looking at my guide:
Bellevue. A fortress with a fine view thrown wide
On Paris—palace of Gallic fantasy—
On Paris—and some places further away . . .
As you lean forward on your scarlet rim
How quaint to you (who) "probably" must seem,
As you look from your boundlessly high spheres,
All our Bellevues and our Belvederes!

I skip. Inconsequence. Expediency.
The New Year's at the door. With whom shall I
Drink toasts, to what? With what? In the foam's place,
A cotton wad. What for? It strikes—my role in this?
What am I to do in all the din of New Year,
With the internal rhyme of "Rainer—died there"?
If you, if such an eye's snuffed out, in truth
It means that life's not life and death's not death.
It means it's darkening, when we meet it'll dawn,
No life, no death—new, third phenomenon,
For 'twenty-six (bedding 'twenty-seven in straw),
What a bliss to end, for 'seven to start with you!
Across the table that the eye can't glimpse,
Will we drink toasts with quiet resonance
Of glass on glass? No barroom sort: the chime
Of I on *you* which fuse to give a rhyme:
Third, new.

　　　　　　　　Over the table I look at your cross.
How many places out of town, such space
Out here! To whom do bushes wave their boughs
If not to us? These places specially ours,

Not others'! All the leaves! The needles, too!
Places of yours with me (of you with you).
We could have made a rendezvous there, just
To talk. Not only places! But the months!
And weeks! And rainy suburbs, streets with never
A soul! And mornings! And all this together,
And not struck up by any nightingales!

I'm in a pit, so likely my vision fails.
You see more up there, above, that's probable.
Nothing has worked out for us at all.
So purely and so simply nothingness
To fit with our capacity and size
That there's no need for me to list it. Not
A thing, except—do not expect the out-
Of-line (I can't, in truth, say out-of-time)
And anyway, into what norm, what line
Would it fit? One old refrain we sing:
"Nothing can be made out of no-thing."
O for something, even shade of shadow play!
Nothing at all: that house, that hour, that day.
Even a prisoner in chains, in death row's grips,
Endowed with memory has: those lips!
Or have we looked too long, hard for a cure?
Of all *that* only *that light* was ours for sure,
As we are only the reflection
Of us—in place of this—*that world* beyond!

In the least built-up outskirt of them all,
Happy new place, Rainer, world, Rainer!
At the far cape of the demonstrable,
Happy new vision, Rainer, hearing, Rainer.
To you all was an obstacle:
Passion, even friend.
Happy new sound, Echo!
Happy new echo, Sound!

MARINA; OR, ABOUT BIOGRAPHY

How often on the schoolroom chair:
What's beyond the mountains? The rivers, there?
Are they pretty, those landscapes without tourists?
Is it true, then, Rainer—heaven's mountainous,
With thunder? Not just the heaven in widows' prayers,
It's not the only heaven, above it there's
Another? With terraces? The Tatras make it clear
That heaven can't be other than an amphitheater
(A curtain lowered over someone, too . . .)
That God's a Baobab, Rainer, is it true,
A *growing* tree? And not a Louis d'Or—
God's not alone—but over him's one more
God?

      How's your writing going in your new place?
If you're there, so is verse, in any case.
How's your writing in the good life to come
With no desk for your elbow, for your palm
No brow—

      In your usual script, send some lines!
Rainer, are you pleased with those new rhymes?
For—to interpret *rhyme* in its truest sense,
What's death if not a whole new range, expanse
Of rhymes?

      Impasse. The language's studied through.
A whole new expanse of new sense, and of new
Assonances.

      —Till we meet! Are friends!
I don't know if we'll meet, but our songs will blend.
Happy new world, even for me wrapped in mystery—
Happy whole sea, Rainer, happy whole me.
Scribble ahead a few lines—so we don't miss.
Happy new tracery of sounds, Rainer.
In heaven there's a ladder up it with Gifts . . .
Happy new hand-position, Rainer!
I cup my glass with palm, so they can't pour me one,

Above the Rhône—and high above Rarogne,
Above pure and simple parting and
Deliver this to Rainer Maria Rilke's hand.

Translated by David McDuff

■ □ ■ □ ■

"My poems are a diary, my poetry a poetry of proper names," says Marina.

Marina is sitting on a round hill, smoking.

I travel through the years with just one suitcase. Time—remembrance, cursed biographies. Where am I traveling? Toward her, toward myself, into some other country?
Glancing neurotically at the timetable does not help me at all.
I yearn for Marina. A Russian poet, born 1892, committed suicide in Yelabuga, 1941.
What really happened? The loss I feel, one reason for writing?

My memory: a tapering funnel. At its end where it touches the darkness sits a child-tree, drawing. I lay bare, not the minute which has just past, but days, years.
The tree is a child's tree, I say in a drone into the funnel. I place my hands around my lips and shout from here, from this Berlin summer of 1983. It's hot, but I've put on thick black woolen stockings. Am I already feeling the cold like Dora, the young actress who no longer leaves her room?

Dora, Marina, and I. Three women saying farewell. Or arriving somewhere, where the sun still shines.

The suitcase means travel. But where to? Back to Zagreb again? For the tenth time only for a visit, inadmissibly brief.

MARINA; OR, ABOUT BIOGRAPHY

Am I nothing but a traveler and therefore already a foreigner? Marina left Russia too. That was in the twenties. I finger various biographies. And I wonder where we went wrong.

In 1950 I am standing indecisively beside my friend in a small apartment in Zagreb. He is stretching felt over a wooden mold with the help of short nails. He taps them with a hammer. The slippers he is making are gray, their felt soles black and ugly. A poet and a shoemaker. They don't sell well, and even I don't wear them around the house. At the trade fair, in the sun, they look so wintery that scarcely anybody stops in front of those five pairs he has set out on a white sheet. All that remains is a picture. (Is it inaccurate? I never went with him to the fair.) And the fact that the room smelled of glue. There were books lying on the table, papers, there was a little food in the fridge. That picture, thrown over the room, turns it into a solid lump. That unknown man in it was my friend. Did I guess even then that our life together would not succeed?

We were imprecise, there were assumptions everywhere. He as a child in the school dining room, his mother a cook. The shame he felt. I never actually saw the child he was. I saw only tables, on them bowls of soup. Because that is what he talked about: his shame. It wasn't possible to learn anything real about that time. During our friendship I saw only a deserted school dining room. Empty pictures. Slippers lying in dust in the sun.

Inaccurate words destroy sensuality. I don't possess any memory of his body.

Are biographies merely a world of pictures?

Marina, I would like to do more than simply see.

Yesterday, here in this room in Berlin, I saw the angel of death again.

A woman with two faces, a light one and a dark one, came

into the room. She was strangely cheerful. I used to laugh with Dora once too. That was before she forgot me. And she no longer recognizes me. Just as she does not know the location of the room she no longer leaves. The room is on Ilica Street, in Zagreb. The angel of death in Berlin laughed as well. How does one deal with illnesses—with the sun?

In other words: nevertheless, travel. Do places alter even memory?

As a child Marina had music and words. And summer in Tarusa by the River Oka. She had a mother whose dying words were: I regret only music and the sun. I don't know whether Marina drew as a child. The child I was drew a tree. Always the same one. A straight trunk, a bushy top, red apples in the green. I always drew the same nontree. It was just a sort of involuntary repetition springing from the conviction that I could not in any case draw beautiful trees, the ones in fairy tales. I betrayed the painter in me even then. No confidence. There was no battle waged. I kept on drawing stupid copy after copy of my first tree. I was five years old. No one gave me confidence in any other kind of beauty. Only the satisfaction of imitation. And the tree from the fairy tale? Who was it in the closed room who nourished my inability, my cowardice? Was it those eternal children's books from our grandmothers, our parents, which are eternally inherited and which lie about the rooms of our world? And which are never thrown away? I would keep taking paper and paints and sitting down at the little child's desk. I drew for hours, days, that same nontree. Always red apples, greenery. Lack of imagination and nausea. After that I just scribbled. Stared sullenly at my pencils. Impotence. Fury. When the green tip broke I did not take another pencil, blue or yellow. Green and red. Standing in one spot immobilized. For how long? The sun is yellow, the sea is blue. I learned all that obediently and obediently repeated it. The desire to draw and with it always nausea. I did not emerge from that pattern even at fifteen. People are good and bad. Daddy is tired. Trees are green. Those sentences revolved in me lethargically like a millstone through the long afternoons of childhood. Deadly boredom, pencil chewing. Then turn over the paper with the stupid tree. Draw another one, I'm already six, seven years old. Everyone thinks I'm going to become a painter. Everyone thinks I can see. The dwarf-child which they are nudging along, bringing up, slowly becomes blind. It keeps on drawing its nontree, that is all it possesses. And later it will immediately recognize all tree-children, it will know the source of their reluctance, their mistrust. And so the model of the tree reigned in all areas. Silk ribbons for the hair are pink. No bad weather ever made them fade. Pink. And so now I like wearing black. And again I am not free.

Because it is a question of freedom. We cannot escape from the chrysalis of the child-tree just like that, when we begin really to draw. I no longer believe that, I have done it long enough. I do not know how to draw. I had to accept that. Later I liked painters, I admired them. I sniffed the smell of oil paints as though they held the meaning of life. But the old picture stayed with me a long time. That reluctance where I found myself as in a child's room. That was what childhood was like. It was pleasant, because I was stupid. But to draw the same tree for the hundredth time was a terrible act. A ritual which prevented everything else, the defensive wall of a bourgeois interior, a tiny senselessness. For days, for years. It was an act of security, no risk at all, mere repetition. So conversations about money hit children in the face. And what does your daddy do, child? A tree, a tree, I amused myself maliciously. And went on drawing, trees, Daddy, Mummy. I chewed all the pencils, then I turned to princesses. Blue dresses, hundreds of blue princesses, always with identical faces, little dots for eyes, red lips, line noses. An agony of nausea. The impossibility of escape. I stared impotently at that nonworld on paper. (I had a sketch pad by then.) I stared at those works of my hands and when I wept over them for the first time, furiously, aloud, dismayed, the false dream slowly left my hand and I dared *only* sketch. Such destruction of paper was soon forbidden me. I was left without paints, they didn't buy me any more. Finished, over, she'll never be a painter. Only a tree-child.

And that other tree, when, how soon, and by whom was it torn up, stifled, and later uprooted?

I forgot the slippers.

The literary room of my young poets' marriage quickly drove them away. I threw myself into the study of art. Z.'s loves (my husband was studying literature) became mine as well. Dalí, Magritte, Breton, Éluard. 1953, Zagreb, a room on the fifth floor of a gray building, a dusty balcony with no flowers. I never stand on it, I'm afraid of heights. But there is no body, even in the loud beating of rugs that penetrates into the room through the balcony door. Only the soul is sought, I run after it, I run with it. After African art, surrealism. Z., who has been married once already, talks about love, about nonbourgeois freedom. Did I listen to him, was I able to? Or was there still a schoolchild with a rosary kneeling in me?

Marina met her husband in 1911 in the Crimea. She was eighteen, he was seventeen. On the large beach, where semiprecious stones were often washed up, she uttered the following pledge: If this boy finds my favorite stone, I shall marry him and I shall never leave him. And it happened. On the very first day Sergei Efron brought her a cornelian he had found in the sand. Was this simply a romantic act? Blue sea, a handsome, pale, tubercular boy, her favorite stone? No, for her it would be more than that, it would be a gold, an iron ring already wound around the future. Wearing it, Marina would write, Marina would perish. A swift decision which sought, like every love, to anticipate forebodings of death. Merely a blind decision, spoken with closed eyes? No, she knew what she was doing and she was brave, she knew the future. For she wanted what was least possible: faithfulness. She wanted a ring, and with it death. "I have already experienced everything, taken everything, in my thoughts. My imagination always rushes ahead of me," wrote Marina on 18 April 1911. On 5 May 1911, she arrived in Koktebel and met Sergei Efron on the beach. The story about the cornelian is nice, because it can be told. But there is a riddle behind that story, in Marina's attitude to words, to the given word, as to the written word. She cannot betray words. Or people.

The word is life. It is the beginning.

And in it upbringing, family, homeland.

Which bell do we always respond to? In our house the word *devil* meant sin. Devil—bell—sin. It was not like that for Marina. She loved the devil which sat on the bed in her half sister Valeria's room. She loved him against the world of her mother, her nanny, against the world of religion. There was nothing terrible about it, he sat and she stood in front of him, she loved him. Right up until her marriage Marina would not be able to go into her sister's room without secretly casting a quick glance toward the bed, although it was a long time since the devil had sat there. Or perhaps, nevertheless? ("The house is lo-ong since taken away, even the legs of the bed are no more, but he is sti-ill sitting there.") Reading this story, many years later Valeria was to say: "What? The devil in my room? What nonsense!"
Only love can reconcile us to what we fear. Marina knew that when she was seven years old, Valeria never.

The angel of death in our room yesterday should also be loved. But I was disturbed by its two faces, the dead one under the live one. Torn between being afraid and forgetting my fear, I did not know what else to do but take on the role of protector. That is why I speak to the angel with a tight throat. Her (his) husband treats her (his) illness as we do: inexactly. We protect her but reproach her at the same time. And her husband believes that if it weren't for her illness, he would now be sitting in the bright sun of the island of Brač and he would be a different man. But he does not dare travel with her. Yesterday she was cold so I gave her a woolen shawl. Is this present coldness of mine, my thick black stockings, only a consequence of that fear? To describe all this, but not to touch it: I am becoming more and more pinched, and I am governed by worry instead of by love. I know this already from our father. We reacted to his illness wrongly as well, we did not know how to live with it, we were afraid. For a long time we interpreted his hunger for life, that other face, as strength, we put our trust in it. I put on my black stockings to warm me too late. And the angel of death is now lying far from me in a bed somewhere. As is Father. I see three cypress trees at the Mirogoj Cemetery in Zagreb. Have mercy, angel, and come again. I shall look you in the face and I shall not change. Together let us count on the sun. Escape to the island of Brač, warm yourself differently than you can here in Berlin. No bed, no shawl can warm you as can that stream of light from a baking wall. Leave this deceptive security, collected things, phantoms of salvation. And come again, so that she may leave at last.

We used once to sit on that island of Brač with the painter Stančić on the lower terrace of his house. His face was swollen, we were waiting for the results of tests, his blood count, from the clinic. The sun was shining above our heads, and the cones in the pine trees were bursting open with loud cracks. In spite of the heat, Stančić was wearing a black sweater over his white shirt. The white skin of a painter. And silence. I was thinking of my father whose face had also swollen when he developed cancer. Later, when I dared, I used to feel everyone if I thought they had some thickening on the neck. I am obsessed with that picture: swollen, painful skin. Of course I didn't mention this to Stančić. We sat for a long time like that, then we waited in the quiet white kitchen. His hands on the table. We were waiting for the judgment. (That year was the first time we had spent our summer holiday in his house on Brač.) We could hear the sea, there was a smell of resin. In the studio on the first floor there were quantities of unfinished paintings. Did he already know then? The table was empty, he did not drink even water. The tiles gleamed in the sun. The results that arrived at midday were still good. Relax, throw yourself into hope. He ate again, laughed. Melita brought coffee, we made plans for the evening, for new paintings. But nevertheless, that white kitchen one afternoon on the island of Brač remained in me as the beginning of an intimation of the end. Together with the scent of the pines, a sense of danger stole in. Is it true that since then the pine no longer exists for me? Is it possible only as it was up to then? The loud crack of the cones together with that swollen face? Those are questions about the pathways words take. Or more exactly, about the pathways of the loss of all imprecise content. Everything that is remembered alters the world from the point when something occurred.

Pines, a face, fear.

Marina, a stone-pearl, love.

The pearl-Sergei for her was love without betrayal. He was that always, even when she loved others, when his weakness became a burden. I see that beach and a girl with green eyes. She is smoking and foreseeing the future. And the pearl was not a find, but fate. Without that day in 1911 the word *pearl* on her lips, in her poems, cannot be understood. But then how is it possible to converse at all? Words are the universe of life, a flock of stars which converge and understand each other intuitively. And our misunderstandings lie in the hurried time of nontalk, in the description of facts, in the world of dates which take from us everything that has been. They lie in our blind belief in facts.

There is a biography of words. And that other, cursed one, of events.

I should like to pause and truly forget that this is paper and that these are typed letters. I should like to forget all questions about facts. I should like to accept that for me the letters *p i n e* spell death, but that there are thousands of other pines. False definition through words—are these questions for a biography?
"I am innocent before the last judgment of words," says Marina Tsvetayeva. And accepts responsibility.

Does geography really alter memory? My book in the suitcase, *The Silk, the Shears,* written in Berlin, changes in Zagreb and becomes porous. Some other memory creeps in between the letters. Truth, accuracy, a foreign land. And what else? Are there places for luxury and places for indigence? Apart from place, does the past which lies over the experience also determine our choice and memories? I cannot free myself from the horror that the open suitcase in a Zagreb room suddenly contains a different book. Not untruthful, but different.

Pictures from a distance, a picture of my mother, a picture of Z. And when I'm in Zagreb I really do see them and the distance from remembrance is reduced with the speed of light-years. The living picture arouses other memories too. Photographs from my childhood, letters, family memories rain down on me. In the empty foreign land, I remembered the past. Here, I see it. Had I written the book in Zagreb, it would have been a different book. This realization irritates me and at the same time excites me: For biography as a developing thing is also liberation. Liberation in the face of the terrible: This is how it was.

Change is life.
Solving the riddle is the end.

I now look at the photograph of Marina as a child as though it were my own. The germ of any kind of description lies more in that decision than in knowledge of facts. Our knowledge is often fed on various stories told by parents and other people, the holes and hollows that we fill, rags from different times stitched together. To find oneself is as difficult as seeking the child Marina.
The truth is only in the text itself.

A white dress with a sailor's collar from 1935, its stiff linen, reaches the level of reality which I betray if all I do is remember and rush on, in my search for something hidden. Has this pretty little dress, which I put on with my heart thumping out loud, remained just as indelible as the beatings with the child's yellow cane? Were beauty and pain as they seemed to us when we dragged ourselves, wet, out of the lake of our upbringing? When do we really fall through the net which a family or a country has thrown over us?
All children receive food and ideology.
I think that I have sometimes failed in describing food.

Without a band around the memory which contains what is neither the present nor proximity, words acquire no weight: They are unredeemed in me as I sit here and write. Then, that moment is crammed full only with the remains of various sentences, with the everydayness which I live. For the imagination leans in various ways on the easel of the day, it cannot, it does not always want to soar.

Into the distance, into form, into stories told to others.

The text opens and wells up only when I do not injure it with the imagination's ready-made models.

Recently, a long conversation about the melancholy of bourgeois women. And about the fact that, whatever we offer or do, we cannot help at all. Hence also the coldness of melancholy. A life lived in images. This brings destruction, the loss of reason, death, and nothing is changed. A little art, a little love, a little life, says the painter Charlotte Salomon. And she draws little girls in rooms in various towns. She draws right up to 1939 when the Germans find her in occupied France and send her to a camp, where she dies. The pictures remain, more than seven hundred pictures of melancholy in her family.

At fifteen I am sitting in a room in Buconjić Street with my mother. No, I am not sitting but standing, talking to her. It is only now that I discover that we never sat together, never conversed. So, I am standing and we are not talking, I am telling her how it was at school. I must be telling her something funny, because no one is interested in what we learn or do not learn. At the end of the year my parents merely glance at the report, confident in advance that everything has gone as they expected. I never dared not to fulfill those expectations. So I am standing in the room, and Mother is putting or not putting something into a cupboard, listening, or not listening. Inattentiveness, the melancholy of non-concentration. I stand and lethargy drifts through the room. No interest in anything at all. Only that senseless bustling around some cupboard or table. Beneath the uneasy surface of senseless bustle slumbers fear. Of what? Don't just stand there, set the table, Father will be here any minute, tell Marica to heat the soup, bring the bread, go and see what your sisters are doing, bring the blue glasses, this afternoon you have to go and fetch the shoes from the cobbler's, where are the napkins, put Father's mail on his desk, did you really dust in here, I saw a nice dress for you, don't ride your bicycle so fast, give the washbasin in the bathroom a quick clean, where can Father be, bring me a handkerchief, it's on the bed, how was it at school, did you know all the answers, run to the kitchen and bring a jug of water, the tablecloth isn't exactly clean, but it'll do for today, where are the napkins for your sisters, have you washed your hands, bring me a needle and thread, hurry, go on, run, stop, fetch, don't dream, wretched child! Flustered, absentminded, not at all stern. I quickly learned to cope with this fragmented speech, I did this then that, too much, too little, but in any case it made me overhasty, overslow, tense. I functioned like a clockwork doll, nothing else was offered. That time—a nightmare of melancholy. My father raised his eyebrows, and immediately there would be tears in my mother's and sisters' eyes. And, constantly, that mindless antlike rushing through all the rooms, through the garden and the streets. It was the anxiety of the lost. All the pores of time were stuffed up with dusters, towels, napkins, and loud lamentation. Childhood as in a baby carriage rushing uneasily through the apartment. Where could it have been rushing? Everywhere lay handkerchiefs wet with women's tears. That made me early on forbid myself to weep, my eyes became dubiously dry, I wandered through thick books, searched for a way out, different people, I refused that rain and acquired an apparently smooth skin. I see myself standing in a storm which was not that. I draw my sisters into a corner of the room and cuddle them secretly. I make sure that nothing will provoke my father's fury. At twelve I have a pain in my stomach for the first time, just before lunch. I have to lie down. Or did I have a stomachache so that I could lie down? My sisters have their own room where they can play. I sleep in the living room, the room of all ritual activities. When lunch is fin-

ished, I have to set the table for dinner. And then for break-
fast. There is no other content to bourgeois interiors. The
family table as the myth of a society. The eating room.
Hence my passionate love of my friends' kitchens, of all
kitchen tables at which I shall later dare to eat.
Marina never wrote about eating rooms. Her superiority in
that regard is unattainable for me.
Crockery, cutlery ring forever in my ears. And fear. Because
that one form of family assembly always meant Father's stern
questions about school, and my replies which were stupid.
Lunch, questions, his fury. I endeavor to forget the white
tablecloths of childhood, and run in panic out of the apartments in which people are constantly lying in wait for me.

Much of what I can do today depends on whether I do not
have to remember.

They assemble us like a kind of colored cube. I should like to
be all one color. Only in our dreams does the cube sometimes fall to pieces. Not to put its individual pieces back
together, that is freedom on the threshold of death. After
everything, only the night can be gentle. And the flight I
undertook even then. Flight to where?
For a long time I was mistaken about the kind of flight.

The secondhand-book shop where my first husband worked
was one such place. Full of darkness, books, and dust. The
remains of food lay on paper in the backroom. The paper
was gray too. I used to leaf through the books there and I
realized I had read nothing yet. I was twenty-two years old. I
squatted on the floor beside a pile of books and listened to
Z. explaining to an old woman that he didn't wish to buy her
bad novels. The old woman stood in the shop for a while
longer and then went slowly out into the evening street.
Now there was a boy standing in front of Z. who leafed grim-
ly through the books, pushed them away, taking only one.

He paid the boy five dinars. He yearned for rarities, of course. I was unsure about his criteria. I both did and didn't understand. Must business be merely a temple to the rare? Such questions annoyed him. And I knew, I had been touched in the wrong place again. Senseless feelings for that old woman. Amazement at Z.'s professional coldness, but fear of it as well. Z. was right to think that foolish. But still, the business wasn't going particularly well. So, perhaps an exception could be made? Or what was this buying and selling? I didn't think that was how it should be done. Let those who did believe it be the traders. I liked going to good secondhand-book shops too. Did that mean I had to be capable of running them? Ought I to want to?

There was a copy of Hitler's *Mein Kampf* in the safe. This was the first time I learned that such a book existed. I didn't read it. There was a first edition of Kafka's *Metamorphosis* as well, Leipzig 1915. Then I began to take books home and read them after work. I avoided the shop, its dim light, I avoided Z. leafing through books and pushing them away. When he came home I no longer asked him how the business was going.

Marina read Kafka. Someone has described how, when she was living as an émigré, she was once interrogated in a Paris police station about Sergei Efron's alleged spying activities; instead of replying she simply recited her poems and parts of Kafka's *The Trial*. She said nothing else.

The *simultaneity* of remembrance. The police station building in Paris, a book in the Zagreb shop, accusations, misunderstandings, the same dull light. Is every thread in that fabric equally strong? I pull out threads of various colors. Blue means *sea*.

I am thinking of Marina and writing. She is no longer in the Crimea, she has left Russia altogether, she possessed a ring and followed her husband.

I see Marina in 1926 on the Atlantic coast in Saint-Gilles. Her son Mur is one year old, her daughter Alya thirteen. I see Marina alone on the beach, she is smoking and looking out to sea. The summer has only just begun. Was the air clear enough for her to recognize the outline of the Ile d'Yeu? Was the shore still empty, with no hotels? Was the day showery or sunny? And where was her husband?

Because in her lap lie letters from two poets, from Rilke and Pasternak. A light breeze blows grains of sand from the sheets of paper. Rilke, in his letter of 10 May asks: "Marina Tsvetayeva, Were you not here just now after all? Or *where was I?*" Boris Pasternak writes: "I have begun five letters to you today. . . . I want to live with you, for a long, long time." Was she reading these letters or, with a tight throat, was she listening to the lines of Rilke's elegy:

> Those who love, Marina, they ought not, they must not
> Know so much of perdition. . . .

Did she put the letters in the deep pocket of her apron and then go back to the little room where Sergei was waiting? Or did she stay on the beach for a long time and write there? That "Poem about a Room" for Pasternak which became a poem for Rilke.

A woman on the beach. She writes and foresees the future.

Ten years later Marina would write: "I was Rilke's last joy, his last Russian joy—his last Russia, his last friendship." And Boris Pasternak? She knew that he wanted to come to her. But she would not let him. "I did not want a general catastrophe."

On 6 June 1926 she completed a poem about a room.

> . . . My friend: as in a letter or a dream
> I shine for you in this space!
> As your lids cover your eyes in first sleep
> I am already with you, intimation of the night
> And brightness. And when that time is over
> I am but the gleam of your dark eye. . . .

I should like to travel to Saint-Gilles although there cannot be any traces left there now.

I should like to see that beach, that sea. The house in the poem, the three walls of the room, as she retreated, backward, toward the fourth.

Nothing but lost places. Where the secondhand-book shop was in 1952 there is a café now. Neon lights, espresso machines, cakes on glass shelves.

Today I stand in front of its window, it is difficult to recall the former picture. The picture is possible only in the head. As is Saint-Gilles.

And Dora? She married a man who knew Z. well. But that was much later. In 1952 Dora was still a child and she was not ill. She lived in a town on the coast with her aunt. She had no mother or father. She wore dark socks and a tight clean dress. There was little food and little love for her in that old, decrepit house. She had no dolls, she played with wool and thread. She never ate ham, ham was for the teacher, so that he would notice her among the other children. That was what her aunt thought. They put sugar on her bread. Bread with jam was the greatest desire of her childhood. She recited her first poems at school. She did not yet know she would become an actress.

The biographies of others. Splinters in our body. As I pull them out, I pull out my own pictures from the deep, dark funnel. Whatever I see, I see in my memory. And it always comes with a creeper which I drag with me from the past.

Marina. That name also brings the remembrance of a date. A date in 1941. In a distant country, in the unknown town of Yelabuga, 31 August 1941. Why did a woman have to die that day?

The loss of one person always casts light on the loss of others. Behind the door of my childhood, when I open it, lie piles of clothes, old furniture, damp school exercise books. Words and loud popular songs echo there. Unknown creatures crawl over the whole heap, there is a smell of forgotten rain, wet roads, torn gloves damp with snow, there are coffins there, photographs, silk hair ribbons. It is almost impossible to close the door again, with the weight of that hill pressing against it, all those tablecloths, pianos, beatings, that whole pile is bursting through it. Wordlessness and memory. I lean my back against the hill, spiders run over my hands, old rags wind around my legs, and in the end I give up, I sit down in the middle of it all.

Doors of youth, doors of women's lives. And behind the doors always untidy rooms, children's shouts, crumpled beds; no time to come to ourselves. And art is a brilliant star in the white, clean rooms of men, shut in books with gold letters, in heavy monographs, in spaces where there is nothing but a writing desk. And those other men, our allies? It is often hard for them. And so my heart increasingly belongs to those of them who, in poorly lighted kitchens, place a saucepan or frying pan on the cooker with a swift, sure movement.

When Marina passes through the room (and she would if she still existed), she always has paper, a pencil, and a notebook in the deep pocket of her apron. And I hear her words: "I have settled completely into my notebook."

Dora sits in a house in Zagreb and says nothing anymore. Her spirit left that room five years ago. And where did I move to? Was it only to another country? A divided life, a bit in Zagreb, a bit in Berlin, one part devours the other.
Perhaps one of the questions is: What is stronger, memory or assumptions about memory? "I have settled completely into my notebook." The beauty of a truth without a picture.

It is said that traveling players are dying out. Perhaps rooms or notebooks are our stages today. For landscapes rightly flee from our habitations. Or they are raped. Dazzling beams of light seek us from high watchtowers, and no longer from theater footlights. That has changed. But I too have the opportunity to move into my notebook. What happened on 31 August was connected with that. Concrete cities stifle poets.

Kafka writes on 30 November to Felice:

> They can't drive me altogether out of writing as I have already thought several times that I am sitting in its midst, in its best warmth.

Felice Bauer lived in Wilmersdorf Street in Berlin, a few steps from the building where I am writing this. Her house was destroyed in the war, now there is a department store selling men's clothes where it stood. Places for flight and passing through. Berlin. The crossroads of biographies. Marina and Kafka could have met. In 1922 she left Berlin for Prague, in 1923 he moved from Prague to Berlin. Somewhere, on some street, on some train, at some railway station they could have seen one another. In Berlin Kafka lived in Grunewald Street, he considered that right outside the city: "The main reason, of course, is that there at the zoo, when I come out of the underground station I lose the ability to breathe and immediately start coughing. Then I am more afraid than usual and I see all the threats of the city united against me. . . ." Marina lived with her daughter Alya in a hotel on Prague Square in the center of Berlin. There she met Andrey Bely who lived in Zossen, also outside the city. Many years later in her prose piece "Captive Spirit" she was to describe that meeting with him and what he said to her:

> . . . "How do you like it here? I don't like it. I . . . don't know why but I don't like it. . . . I didn't like it from the start, from the moment I got here. . . . And when I left— I didn't like it. They told me Berlin had wonderful surroundings. . . . I was expecting . . . something like Zveni-

gorod. . . . But here . . . it's somehow—naked! Have you noticed the trees?" (I hadn't noticed them at all, because spindly bushes with protective bars around them can hardly be called trees.) "There are no shadows! There's a German legend about a man without a shadow, but that was a man—trees must cast shadows. And the birds don't sing here either. How could they—in such trees! In Moscow they used to sing to me every morning, they sang even in 1920, they sang even in the hospital, even during the typhus epidemic. And the population is repugnant. So suspiciously quiet. They walk as though they had cloth soles. Haven't you noticed? And then— they are all dressed in black. Not a single person in brown or gray, all in black, even the women."

(To myself: Ah, my dear, hence your passion for my blue!)

"And their furniture is white, it all smells of new wood. There is something (he shudders) ominous in that. Perhaps this is a special kind of settlement?"

I answer quickly:

"No, no, after wars it's like this everywhere."

He, evidently relieved:

"Oh, I see! You mean—widows and widowers? A special settlement for widows and widowers. . . . Oh, how German . . . how Prussian that is. . . ."

Bely died in 1934 from the effects of sunstroke. Marina believed that he had died of "sun arrows," as he had written prophetically in a poem in 1907:

I believed in golden rays
And died from arrows of the sun. . . .

A giant was standing in the shop full of old books in Zagreb one evening. He had a green cavalry twill coat, his face was pale, his hair dark. His full, almost feminine lips were striking. He was holding papers in his hands, monotypes, on which embracing bodies were drawn. Those four pages were illustrations for a book of my husband's poems. The two of them discussed the size of the edition, paper, and costs. The book was to be called *There Is No Dream That Can Take Your Place,* and the painter was curious about the title. His sharp glance merely grazed me, and then he smiled. His hand was dry and soft. Later Stančić would say that I didn't notice him at all on that occasion. But that isn't so. It isn't so because he quickly took a piece of bread from his coat pocket and began to eat it. I remembered that, and that he talked for a long time about hunger. He pushed his hat up with his index finger, his coat sleeves were torn. His drawings were very beautiful. He lived as a subtenant in one room, in which he painted, and in which his pregnant wife slept. He brought water from a pump on the square. He invited us to visit him one evening. There were dead lovers on the title page of the book. Later Z. told me, he's a surrealist, you know. I did not know. I began to read Breton, to look at Dalí's paintings. I liked the picture of the melting watches best.

Paul Klee called one of his paintings *The Carpet of Memories.* He too saw his memory as a fabric with fine patterns woven into it.

The round hill where Marina sits is a hill of vanished, discarded, lost things behind the doors of childhood. We two are linked by things which were borne away.

During the war, in the summer of 1941, the black piano was suddenly in the eating room. Our family had moved from Belgrade to Zagreb and my grandmother, Father's mother, arrived from somewhere as well. She used to come to lunch on Sundays, and in the afternoon she would play Chopin waltzes on the piano. Grandmother played loudly, with a lot of pedal, the whole room resounded. I don't know whether she played well, but she began to give me my first piano lessons. She had no experience in this and for some time we tortured the keys together with Czerny exercises. From the start I had to play for two hours a day, Father sat beside me with a watch in his hand. That practice seemed endless, I made no progress at all.

Then Father found a real teacher for me and I ran to him on Bosanska Street twice a week. He lived in a small house with his mother and sister. I was to get to know the sister better later, and in 1976 she hanged herself in that house. My hands were small and the new teacher did not believe I would ever play well. Then Father sent me to a friend with whom he often played cards. This friend was a very well known pianist, the famous brother of the famous Zinka, and later he became her co-repetiteur. Now I went to a house in Dolac, beside the market and, while I stumbled awkwardly through the exercises I had been given, Mr. Kunz would run agitatedly through the whole apartment. It must have been painful for him. Mr. Kunz often had to make telephone calls during lessons, he had visitors, corrected me distractedly, and then disappeared somewhere. And so nothing came of it all. He had no other pupils, he taught me only because of my father and I did not learn much, always interrupted by his telephoning and other everyday trifles. He kept going into the kitchen, drinking coffee for a long time, forever searching for something among his papers on the desk, holding long conversations with his other sister, whose beautiful, gentle, red-haired portrait hung above the crockery cupboard, while the picture of the other, famous sister, a plump beauty, stood in a gold frame on the piano. Outside the window was the activity of the market-place, peasants, German soldiers, townspeople. No one talked about the war. It was not noticed in those rooms with pianos, and the protégée, over whom people were so concerned and concerned themselves so little, who was already attending the secondary school run by nuns (blue tunic, white socks), this protégée was a sad disappointment. She was accused of being unmusical. That went on until 1945 when there was suddenly no money in the house anymore and when, almost as a punishment, Father sold the piano. Despite the fact that he had two other daughters who might have been better at piano than I was. But no, in this new phase music no longer made any sense to him. That piano, which had not acquired a single scratch throughout the whole of the war, became superfluous in the proletarian phase. I did not regret losing it at all. I was fighting for my green bicycle, Father wanted to sell that too.

Married just a short time, Marina lived on Gleb Boulevard in Moscow. Her apartment was arranged like a kind of past. All the rooms as they had been once in her childhood. Instead of the black piano, on which her mother, Marina, and her sister Asya had once played, there was a brown piano in the apartment, the one from the summerhouse in Tarusa. The pictures on the walls hung just as they had in that house. The table, chairs, everything was simply a repetition of that former apartment.

Still no life of your own, Marina? A young woman yearns for the past and repeats what has been. She does not want to lose her childhood. Her first child arrives, her daughter Alya, but she is still a child herself. Retain it, nurture, strengthen. The replica of the apartment on Gleb Boulevard was the dream of a loss transformed into reality. In it lived also those who had died, involving themselves in everything: what an embroidered tablecloth should look like, where the sofa should stand, the books, the old guitar. The same, fanatical loyalty again. Marina knew, forgetting is a sin.

Through the windows of the other apartment she moves into Marina looks out at poplars. Or does she see only the River Oka in Tarusa? In the rooms hang pictures, oval, round, small, large. Many faces. The wallpaper has floral patterns, the chairs are covered with velvet. Marina's mauve blouse. There is still hope, she is young.

I didn't save much from my childhood. Two or three pictures, a couch, some crockery. The books, the black furniture, the carpets, the stamp collection, the sewing machine, were all sold in 1945. Our apartment was arranged in bourgeois style, and in any case I had wanted for a long time to escape from life in the eating room. From the card playing, dances, celebrations. From the cold kitchen. And so I did not find it at all difficult to part early from our undeservedly good life during the war. No dream of any landscape, no landscape whatever ran in my veins, was left in my blood. Childhood was a time of imprecise fear, a dull beating of the heart, I did not want to retain any of it.

Splinters of happiness, Marina, that life afterward.

The loneliness before that sentence is different, warm. She, Marina, is not yet lying cold on the bed in Yelabuga. And there is no white anywhere. In my head, amazement. Didn't anyone pray? Were the little windows of the house really closed? What was the sky like over the town? The roads were swimming in water, there were boards lying where the puddles were deep. Shoes, clothes, spattered. Darkness around the wooden house, three small windows in front, a low roof. An old fence, two trees in the garden.

And the room, the color of the walls, the height of the door? Flickering light from the street lapped lazily over her body. That body was hanging. No notebook of poems in the deep pocket of her gray apron. That no longer existed. It was 1941.

To drive away the pictures from that unknown night: cut memory off. All the threads between the years. The times were cold. But still they were an example of a model existence and my pitiful lethargy. A woman who will not die, that's how I see you. Because you existed, because you exist as words. As a feeling, handwriting and permanence.

Marina as a child. She is wearing a suit from the beginning of the century. I would not like to press the cap, which I put on her head in 1983, onto her hair in order to materialize a description which is no longer possible in this way.

Is there any way of seeking? A woman, women, the world in my head?

Our happiness in splinters, Marina, that life afterward. Shreds, of rationality, of discovery.

We are composed also of lives that have passed. With this realization it is possible to fly away from here, from this gray zone of Berlin. It is possible to move along other roads, to stand behind the low fences of a suburb of Prague or in Meudon (the sounds of planes and cars here immediately retreat), it is possible calmly to accept predicted losses. And so take up residence in the imagined. Because we must live somewhere.

It is possible to observe foreign, alien places.
Berlin 1966. The Film Academy on Pommerns Street. I was thirty-six years old. Berlin 1922, Marina Tsvetayeva is living with her daughter Alya in a hotel on Prague Square. The Film Academy was the most foreign place in my life. Corridors lit by neon lights, shiny, cold walls. The young students were spoiled in a way that was new to me. They were arrogant and sexless, the illusion of film was everywhere, nothing but a rapid life in pictures. But we did not create it, that other reality. During the projection we ate dry rolls of noncommunication. There was no answer to many questions and in 1968 many of the students were completely immersed in politics. Those three years of study poured down my spine leaving an icy track. My heart closed, my eyes like holes without lids stared at the white screen before the film. The course about the popular films of the Third Reich shattered the last possibility of belief in new images. Everything was glued together with already familiar scenes, with false emotions and political exploitation. The power of the images made them suspect. The word *imagination* was prohibited. Because the images had to chase only after consolation, of that childish, film variety. But if what retains, holds, is lacking, then time is trans-

formed into the fluent unwinding of events and thereby into nontime. Traces of the truth are destroyed and the images elicit a response only by means of technique, which then controls them. Soon I had no one left to talk to and I retreated into books again. When the students began to dream about Hollywood and success I was already in the third year, and about to leave. I see my erstwhile colleagues from time to time rushing through the city in large black cars.

Marina is in Czechoslovakia, in Všenory, alone. She sits in a tiny room, writing letters. Her daughter Alya is ten years old. Her husband Sergei works the whole day at the university in Prague. He returns home by the last train late at night. "I fill up the time in the morning with the French lessons I give Alya (I spend the second half of the morning cooking and keeping the fire going), I fill up the days with darning—with such zeal—stockings (two pairs of mine, five of Alya's—and analyzing everything, everything!) and so I fill up one more year, perhaps even two—only, onward!" The little room in Vshenory is damp, streams run down its walls in the evening. Marina sits at the table wrapped in all the shawls she possesses and her pen scratches steadily over the paper. So Sergei writes to his friend Chernova in Paris. He is already writing critically about the Russian émigrés in Paris, that foreshadows what happened to him later. Did Sergei have those problems because he was an émigré Jew? Is that one of the reasons for the isolation of the Efron family?

Time gorges itself on our hearts.

And Dora? At first she smoked too much, then she used to drink several glasses of wine each day, then she lay down in the big bed and did not want to talk to anyone anymore. Dora Novak, that talented actress. And so in her hands time was turned into something nonexistent.
The town was, as always in summer, very hot. The house in

which the bed stood, a house dating from the thirties, was near the hospital. The room where Dora lived with her husband was next to his mother's room. She owned everything. The house smelled of power, severity, and good food. Loud music could be heard from the apartment below, in front of the house there was a new car, in the apartment a new radiogram. Everything proclaimed the new age. Gâteaux, vitamins, video. Dora turned over in the big bed and was pleased that she was lying in it in her best dress. She was pleased that she had at last ceased to function, or, as she put it, that she had begun to sin. Under the protection of the family, the town, and the theater.

Once, in the Theater Academy, people had praised her clear pronunciation, she was offered leading roles on television, in the cafeteria men immediately stretched their hands toward her as she passed. But the theater was quickly seen to be a power struggle. The narrow streets with a new generation of girls pushed her up against the gray wall of the building where she had her first room. With numb fingers she shortened her brown skirt which was too long and felt unhappy in that culture. What she wanted to bypass was her former life. There at the coast she had sung out loud by the sea, that was why her aunt had sent her to Zagreb: You're bound to succeed! But how? Could Dora live only from the inside of her being? And she quickly noticed that it was not a question of her voice, but of what the voice could do. She felt the material itself was unusable.

The town with its parks (that pleasant unpleasant heat), was neither large enough nor small enough to accept the girl Dora: It was the south, with a west wind sometimes, she noticed that. The people were often old-fashioned, the new buildings frightened her. Half the provinces wanted to come to that town, or had to if they intended to achieve anything. Dora shut her eyes tight.

Soon she began to feel that everything was a battlefield. People pushed in the streetcars, she was constantly moving, rushing, her skin became tender from so much touching. She wanted only to escape again. At last, her first radio part. She didn't sleep the night before the recording. She spoke her text wearily, almost without any voice. But people liked it. She thought: Yes, everything can be consumed. A man fell in love with her, and she was still young enough to believe she could escape into love, into marriage. She moved into the room next to her mother-in-law's, life as a couple, a threesome. She cooked badly and with difficulty, in the evening she went to work at the theater, she spent herself equally intensively on everything, she had no reserves left. Division of time, division of labor, those were threatening words for her. She escaped into sleep even during the day, she burned meals, lost money at the market. Was this only simulated incompetence, or was it a way out of everything after all? Her mother-in-law's admonitions achieved nothing but increasingly morbid inertia. And so she was driven into a little corner of bohemianism. Full cupboards stood wide open, at night she would get into bed, fully dressed. She accused everyone of treachery, disloyalty, and avarice. She grew wild, began shouting, was on some other planet. And her husband felt that she was biting rebelliously into the core of truth, that she was breaking all her teeth, he was full of understanding, he bore that burden. The compassion of others shattered the remainder.

In bed Dora covered herself with two blankets even though it was summer, she pulled on thick woolen stockings, two or three sweaters, and slowly forgot who she was. Outside the sun slid over the sky, as it once had at the coast, but her heart throbbed with the figures of earnings, wages, expenditure, life. These were figures which sprang up, in every conversation, in every activity. They had lodged in her, she could no longer pull them out. Her husband took over the cooking, the washing, she no longer went to the theater, her face became set. She was a person and she was falling apart. Who said that? Friends gave her husband all sorts of advice. A stay in a clinic. Or: She must get a grip on reality, that's the way life is. No one can stay pure. She's really naive. Her sensitivity, why honestly. We're so sorry for you.

Dora stopped speaking her clear, childlike sentences. Sometimes she went to a café, she watched the people, she no longer heard anyone. The strong plant of resistance bloomed within her. She unhooked herself from life, she spoke through her blood, her skin, she sat absently on a chair and gradually turned to stone. With light steps she attained the freedom of not having to do anything anymore. She did not have to eat, to talk, to cook, to act, to do anything now that in any case nothing existed. Dora is ill, people said in the café, and sighed briefly. They drank their coffee or brandy, went on talking, making plans, thinking up new productions. The chimney of ambition smoked, people chased after success, threw off the provinces. Outside, people talked about prices, bread, politics. In old, dilapidated institutions, people spoke about the way art crosses every frontier. Masks, a dusty stage, applause.

And Dora stayed in bed. A year, two, four. Sometimes she would say something: Would you like some coffee? Yes, you'll have coffee, won't you? Coffee please! Then she would smile and turn her head away.

The summers became increasingly hot, friendships, marriages fell apart, the number of motor accidents increased. The crowded cafés brought people a kind of sleep, there was loud, modern singing, the sea was far away. Dora, a sunken ship, a pale face. She passes through the rooms like an old woman, sits in an armchair, does not look at anything. Only her hair is still black.

Often people only talk about life. And fear. And meanwhile we kill ourselves in one way or another.

The town is no longer waiting for Dora's return. The loud drums do not reach the one who really sings. Over, finished. A person leaves, moves into the unknown, or sits by a window and says nothing. The conquest of the south has begun.

In 1925 Sergei's Prague scholarship is not renewed and the Efron family moves to Paris. At first they live at a friend's, then they find a small, cramped apartment in the suburb of Meudon. The struggle for survival, for writing, begins. Sergei was not a practical person, he was ill and at first he could not cope at all, he earned nothing. Marina's potential was also limited. In a photograph from 1930 she is standing on some steps, her face looks tormented, her expression is vacant. The time of the blue island of childhood, spacious landscapes, the people there, is over. Perhaps her love for Sergei is over too. Marina lives only in the room, between the pans on the stove and her notebook, she never goes into the center of the city, she stays on the edge of everything.

Long before I came to the Film Academy in Berlin I was no longer a student. Zagreb had grown empty, my literary marriage was coming to an end. My father's death in 1960. I go alone to the funeral. Then separation from Z. I was already working for television, writing scripts, poems. In the evening my new friend and I used to sit with Stančić and his wife. And everything seemed like a kind of repetition. In 1966 I packed my things, locked the apartment on Bulić Street. I had been given a scholarship to Berlin. There I soon met B. and stayed. From then on an attempt to live in two countries. Writing in between. And the loss of those who used to read my poems. I quickly took up residence in the warm land of memory. Childhood had passed, youth had passed. And the child-tree. My hand began slowly to seek other signs. Signs of a no-man's-land without color. Signs out of the dark funnel of remembrance.

> *"And as for the consciousness that thinks in images and forms, there will be hardly anyone who, in the end, does not consider his images as his thoughts,"* writes Artaud.

Sergei Efron remains an obscure figure for us. Everyone who has written about Marina Tsvetayeva seems to have forgotten him. And the fact that he may later have become a traitor has ensured that this silence has been maintained to the present day. But was that what really happened? Did Marina (she was anything but blind) live with such a man? In 1914 Marina wrote to Rozanov: ". . . I want to tell you a little more about Sergei. He is very ill. He developed tuberculosis at sixteen. Its advance has been halted, but his whole state of health is poor. If you only knew what a passionate, generous, profound young man he is! (. . .) In the three years—almost three years—of our life together, not a single shadow has fallen over us. Our marriage right up to today is no ordinary marriage, because I haven't changed at all—I love everything and I live everything just as when I was seventeen. We shall never part. Our meeting is a miracle. I'm telling you this so that you won't think of him as a stranger. For the rest of our lives he is completely mine. I shall never love anyone else, there are too many tears and there is too much rebellion in me. It is only with him that I can live as I live—completely freely. No one at all, not one of my friends understands my choice. Choice! Heavens, yes, it's true, I chose!"

Neither her friends in Russia nor those living abroad wanted to accept Marina's choice: a sick man and a Jew. That is the darkness which lies over Sergei. Everything else to date is rumor.

In 1917 Marina's second daughter, Irina, is born in Moscow. Marina lives in great poverty with both her daughters. Sergei is at the White Front. Then no one knows where he is anymore. Marina tries in vain to find out whether he is alive. There is no more food in the town. In 1920, in a children's home, Irina dies. Of hunger. People see Marina in the street in rags. She is dragging a sledge with a sack of rotten, frozen potatoes on it.

How to live? How to write?
The costume of fiction is full of holes.

But before that there was a dream about art.

The painter Picelj still lives on Gaj Street. Thirty years later. His terrace has become still more luxuriant, his studio is painted white, as before. Two rooms, big windows, tiny kitchen. Two marriages, one daughter.
In these rooms the group Exat (Eksperimentalni Atelje) was founded in 1951. Conversations at night with painters, architects, I read my first poems aloud there. ". . . The Exat 51 group sees no difference between so-called pure and so-called applied art . . . it believes that the methods of work and principles in the field of nonfigurative—of abstract — art are not the expression of decadent tendencies, but, on the contrary, it sees the possibility that the study of these methods and principles will develop and enrich the field of visual communications in our country . . . ," stated the catalog of an exhibition in the spring of 1953. Of course some people thought the group was an expression of decadence. Despite these objections, exhibitions were put on and, in a short time, they became very successful. Ivan never had a large following for his paintings. He earned money by designing

books. That's the way it still is. The group lasted for a long time and some of the group joined the New Tendencies movement, founded in the sixties in a restaurant garden above Zagreb. Later, life separated us. Some became famous, some left Zagreb. Only Ivan remained the same always. A vigorous devotee of pure form. He never changed. We drink coffee, as we used to on his terrace. We do not talk about money. He shows us papers given him by Arp.

We crouch on the floor and smoke. And his quiet restraint captivates us.

What I am seeking, Marina, is also lost courage.

At first the painter Stančić did not like the group's paintings. I had to conceal the fact that I used to go to the white studio. The exclusiveness of youth and love. In 1954 Stančić painted my first portrait, in an armchair. He painted over it. He used to paint over a lot of pictures in those days. He was often dissatisfied, and there was no money for new canvas. The paints were bad, they cracked. No one liked his dark paintings as yet. On Sundays we would go to fairs. We would buy dishes or perhaps a dress. For years we didn't wear anything new, friends would possess one coat, one sweater. It was cold in our rooms, we ate too little fruit. Stančić drew vignettes for the daily papers, Z. and I translated a book almost every month. In a corner of the south we were poor and we were sure of the future.

In Všenory Marina is expecting a baby. She lets out the one dress she possesses, complains of the clumsiness of her body. In 1925 her son Mur is born. Is she pleased? Is she afraid of the days that will be spent washing diapers and not writing poems? Now there are four of them, and Sergei loses his Prague scholarship. The family wants to move to Paris, Marina hopes that she may be able to earn more there with her literary work. With one suitcase they leave the damp room in

Všenory. I see Marina, walking heavily, making her way along the muddy lane toward the station. Still full of hope.

"Lucky the one who does not pay for his poem with his life," recites Branko Miljković in the Writers' Club in Zagreb. It is morning, the club is still empty. Branko is wearing a black coat and a black hat. He writes poems which we all love. I don't know why he moved to Zagreb from Belgrade, someone said it was because of an unhappy love. But he says nothing about that as he drinks his brandy at the table, he only recites his poetry. And won't let us go. It's ten o'clock, we're sitting in the club, talking. And, of course, we feel that he cannot be alone that day, we don't know anything more about him, we don't know that he is unhappy. He says nothing about the woman who doesn't love him enough. "Don't kiss the hand of the past." And so we sit in the club, my lips smart from so many cigarettes, we sit until six o'clock in the evening. Then Branko says he wants to go home, he wants to write. We are glad to have met and at once arrange to meet again the next day, we agree on the time and place. He has a room at 11 Bijankini Street. That was the night of 10 February 1961. In the club the next day we see police photographs. He hanged himself that night from a low willow on Ksaver Square. We are shaken, helpless, we run to the square, stand by the willow, silently, our eyes are blind with tears. Could we have helped, prevented this act? But it is no longer and never will be six o'clock again, for us to keep him sitting at that table in the club. It's too late for anything. An acquaintance tells us that Branko did not go home that evening, he drank the whole night, and this was not his first suicide attempt. I don't know whether there was any letter for that unknown woman. The following day, Z. went to Belgrade in the car with the coffin, to the funeral. We placed flowers on the coffin in silence and followed the car with our eyes until it disappeared. Branko was twenty-seven years old. And we used to go to the tree, that low one, every year in

February, as long as the tree was there. While I was in Zagreb, his poems always lay on my desk under the lamp. And I can still see and feel that evening in the club, my smarting lips. And the way he went home to write. It was six o'clock in the evening. And I slept soundly that night.

The past lives in us without chronology. Everything is simultaneously here, all colors, all feelings. As we talk, we often do violence to this simultaneous memory. Every book about life could run parallel, in columns, it could express the whole if we were not brought up to believe in sequences, in hierarchies. Important, unimportant. Beginning, end. This arbitrariness springs from our desire to intervene, to explain. But that is violence too, done to what we have experienced. In that way we have linked ourselves to the external biography, to the junctions.

We have been granted this fabrication about beginnings and ends by our belief in experience, in the march of time, in aging. Physical death as the final point of a story, a life. The past, the future, rising, falling lines. I do not want to write for that death. I should like to repeat Marina's question: Who will break the clock and so free us from time? What we need to find is some other kind of time. We should uncover other sources, the whole surface of remembrance. Let us avoid all choice! For on the shore of such lost time there no longer exist favorite places, and there are no traveling companions.

We ought to try out the text in a stammer, let ourselves blindly down into the dense undergrowth of a being who seeks, sleeps, and does not die. Our hands on the table do not feel only wood, what the hands always remember is more than the table, more than its warmth or coldness, its scratches or smoothness. The rain that was falling then is always present as well, and the words of our friends in the room. The soothing remedies of this age of ours will ruin us. The hour of death or the end, that is untruth.

I write in Berlin, I write on the train, then in Carolinenseal on the North Sea. I write in winter, in a foreign house with foreign noises and an unfamiliar wind. I write even when I am not writing, on the seashore or in the EDK shop where you can buy everything. Except books. I stop helplessly in front of those shelves where everything exists. On the wax cloth on the table, in the foreign house, lie the letters of Marina Tsvetayeva, published in Paris in 1972. The whirlpool of those letters is stronger than the voices of the living around me. "What I feel toward humanity—is either indifference or a whole novel."

I do not write about our neighbor who gave us the keys to the house with the words: "I just want you to know, I was a Nazi!" No, not now. The wax cloth has an extremely pretty pattern of little flowers, the furniture of the living room is impersonally practical. Everything is at hand for a domesticity that is not ours.

Is writing always that other life we do not have? That other half of the day? An inner clock strikes out a different time from the clock on the white wall of the room. We shall lose that time, if we forget.

Marina, on this coast there are no cornelian pearls. I found only a transparent pebble, but it may be just ordinary, polished glass. B. found a lump of tar. And then there were dead birds lying on the sand. We did not see barrels of poison. But still, when I walk on the shore at Carolinenseal, I think of the Crimea. And the picture is clearer than this landscape here. Or more exactly, the picture of the Crimea intrudes into everything. It falls like a curtain in front of the island of Wangerooge and hides it. From now on every sandy shore could be that one in the Crimea. So the deathless may also vanquish that past. The island of Brač is always present as well, the painter who has gone, the swollen face. Everyone's life is made up of vertical remembrance; that is why I often lack concentration in this one, I forget what I have said or what B. has said to me. I wake reluctantly when the everyday dominates, when I cook, talk, eat. Fairness to one love is always also unfairness to another. That love I think of. And loneliness always includes other losses.

As a child Marina loved the devil. She loved him although she knew she should not. That was her first escape from orderly bourgeois life. She would run secretly to the room of the half sister she did not like, her passion was great. Right up until the moment when the devil was no more, when she lost him because she grew up. But that kind of courage stayed with her always. To love what is forbidden or ugly, as they say. They say that blindly, they never ask questions. Children are beaten because of the division of the world into the ugly and the beautiful, later wars are waged for the same reason. The devil taught Marina that children's games, card games, snakes-and-ladders, are dull. It was the devil who taught her the seriousness of life, wrote Marina. And not the angels. He was gray, ugly, defenseless. And everyone was against him. In the grown-up world other laws of love often reign. But that the devil may be more appealing than princesses, that remains unprovable. Only the facts of love count, Marina knew that, she was really impervious to any other kind of seduction.

The child-tree that was me was afraid of the unknown. It tore away the net of the grown-up laws too late. It sat in the room chewing pencils. It sat like that for a long time. And it dreamed only surreptitiously of ugliness, it didn't even notice itself. At first it chose smooth beauty. It imitated, trembled with fury, when the princesses on the paper were not beautiful enough. For a long time it did not believe in its own abilities, it bowed its head before the black mahogany furniture, before the pictures of the Alps on the walls, before the crystal vases, the china deer, the pots of flowers. In the cave-house full of sweet cookies and white tablecloths it collected nothing but colors, it tried to please everyone, so its own ability to see was stifled. It had virtually no chance of choosing a bitter taste instead of one that was honey-sweet. Silk ribbons in the hair, everything must be eaten up, an obedient curtsy. Those were the crutches I had at six years old. The chances of my seeing the devil on my bed were quite slight. Around my head swirled dusters, in front of my eyes lavish dinners, thick novels about love, shelves without any volumes of poetry, fake jewelry on our neighbor's fur coat, the smell of champagne in the rooms. A mindless, senseless life, no faith, no interest in our country, in its people. All that filled the rooms was petty unreason. And those rooms are identical everywhere, they have no geographical particularity, they do not know north or south, or the continents. The same broth everywhere, the same standards, the same taste. The same comfort, an international refuge for child-trees. Here too, through the curtains, I see children's heads bent over papers in the middle of the metric world of these rooms. The patterns of the wallpaper unanimously change the kind of flower on them, dresses alter their length. Organization functions perfectly in the perfect desert. All the doors of the houses are closed. The lawns of the gardens untrodden. And everywhere there are notices of prohibitions, notices of ownership. Beware of the dog, no entry, private property.

The child-tree sat in the prison of the family apartment and thought it was drawing. And if it did manage to get its head out of that noose, it has to thank external circumstances: the virtually complete collapse of that world. That taste of honey clings to the hands for a long time, that indestructible ideology always germinates anew within us, we do not free ourselves easily from those chains, those rooms. We visit the empty places of life too late, we avoid windy crossroads, for a long time we collect the wrong memories, we sing the permitted songs. Until we notice that we are spinning around in the same spot and that we are sinking.

What saves us is the persistence of instinct—just how did it survive?—and the enigma of the emotions.

In the misery of modern, armed times, this salvation is

threatened. Methods of destruction are invented in the comfortable rooms of the West. And people accept everything. Blindly, cruelly, stupidly. Is that the revenge of children who were not permitted to see? Marina's family was artistic. And upbringing was secondary to that. I am aware that for her this meant making way for other dangers. Not dangers, but other living, other dead zones. Because it is a question also of childhood. The child-tree that has been demoralized never waves to me.

I turn over in bed and dream:

I learn that Marina is living secretly in Switzerland. And her sister Asya has come to "Altbuenden" from Russia. B. and I immediately set off to meet her, at last. We soon find the house where Asya is living. The house is high on a hill. Asya and her husband, both without faces, without bodies, greet us pleasantly. Their suitcase is lying not yet unpacked on the bed. In it I see my manuscript about Marina which I sent them. Down below on the slopes one can see the mountain paths, I think about how B. and I could walk here for a long time. I say to Asya: We are sorry we can only stay for a short time. The train back to Berlin leaves at seven P.M. But we shall come again. Asya asks us whether we would rent a room with a bare wooden floor. We laugh, we have a floor like that in Berlin. We rent the room. B. is no longer with us. I say good-bye to Asya, I hurry to the train. B. is probably already waiting for me there. Suddenly Asya's husband, who is seeing me off, says: Marina is here, two doors away. I freeze. He will call her because he trusts me. We stand under a balcony. Marina comes over. Her hair is black, short, she has turned up the collar of her fur coat. She still looks like the photographs taken when she was young. I am surprised, she is so young. I hold her hands, I am excited, I stammer, I tell her that I have translated her poems with Ina. Ina is Russian and she came to Germany in 1925. I tell Marina that two of her books have been published in Yugoslavia, I want to tell her that she is not forgotten. She is solemn, she tells me to write again. And she will read the manuscript that is in Asya's suitcase. We shall meet again when we come back to Switzerland in a month's time. Her husband—not Sergei but some older gentleman—is sweeping the balcony loudly with a stiff broom. I realize that B. doesn't know where I am, or that I have met Marina at last. On the square under the trees I see a yellow telephone booth. Has Marina come out of it? I am anxious because of our train. I say good-bye to Marina in Russian. I run to the railway station. From the hill I see B. below me, behind a fence, he looks very serious. Beside him is a man I do not know. I run, I come closer and closer. The fence had hidden the fact that B. is sitting in a wheelchair. There is white plaster around his legs. Where can he have fallen? Does it hurt? The man pushes the wheelchair quickly toward the station. How shall we get into the train? I see that his trousers have been cut because of the plaster. Now I won't be able to tell him anything about Marina, my joy over her is now inappropriate. Then I'm even more frightened: We won't come back here, because B. can't walk. It was all in vain. I shall never see Asya or Marina again.

It is quiet in the chamber of time, turned toward the past. The whole year 1939 is made up of dark floating islands. It is a year of night.

My father drags me out of bed at midnight to tell me that he is leaving us. My mother is pregnant. I tremble, standing in my nightshirt in the eating room. My father is not leaving us, his face is dark. I am nine years old and I know nothing about the beginning of the war. And nothing about marriage, love, and parting.

Marina is sitting with her son Mur, he is fourteen years old, in the bare room of a neglected Paris hotel. Her husband Sergei and daughter Alya have already returned to Russia. As a result everyone avoids her. Émigrés see her in the street hungry, in torn clothes. After the entry of the Germans into Czechoslovakia, Marina writes one of her last poems: "Oh Czech lands in tears / Oh Spain in its own blood. . . ." In June she will leave Paris with Mur. A long train journey to Moscow, a journey toward the final stopping place. She does not yet know that her sister Asya has been arrested.

In Paris on 23 April 1939, Marina dreamed:

> I'm climbing up a narrow mountain path. The landscape is like Saint Helena. A precipice on the left, sheer rocks on the right. There's nowhere to escape to. Down the path toward me comes a lion. Enormous, with a huge head. I make the sign of the cross three times. The lion crouches on his stomach and creeps carefully past me. I go on. Toward me comes—a camel. With two humps. A large camel, far larger than me. The sign of the cross three times. The camel steps over me. I'm covered by a tent, its belly. I go on. Toward me comes—a horse. It's bound to knock me over the edge, it's trotting. Three signs of the cross. It gathers itself and leaps over me. I'm delighted by the elegance of that leap. Now I'm flying on my back, my head is being dragged off. Below me are cities . . . large at first, with sharp outlines (I'm flying in spirals), then only little heaps of stone can be seen . . . I see mountains, bays. I rush headlong on; with a feeling of terrible sadness and final parting. I feel clearly that I am flying around the earth's globe and that I am clinging to it passionately and hopelessly!—knowing: The next orbit of the universe will be into that complete emptiness I always feared so much in my life. On swings, in lifts, on the sea, within myself. There was only one solace: This was fateful, it could no longer be stopped or changed, and nothing could ever be more terrible.

Her fear of the elevator: That is why she always used the stairs. Her panic at cars, at driving. She could not bear to be shut up in them. Yes, emptiness and movement. Emptiness on a swing, in porches, and everywhere foreignness.

She caught me yesterday on the porch of the house on

Mommsen Street. I was climbing the steps, suddenly I turned a little to the left, took hold of the wooden railing, and felt under my hand the iron railing of the building where I lived in Zagreb. The dusty sun in the Berlin porch suddenly set, and behind the high door of Frau Mueller's flat I saw quite clearly little Mrs. Borić from the ground floor in Zagreb. She was smiling, smoking as usual, and it was many years before her death. She waved to me and time rolled backward and forward. Why was I climbing these steps in Berlin, I wondered, it was not poverty or the search for work that had brought me here. Was it love perhaps?

I was a young woman when I talked with Mrs. Borić, now I am as old as she was then. She did not know how to read and write properly, which caused her great shame. Despite that she held out my first volume of poems to me and asked me for a dedication. I stand on the steps there as here, and awkwardly, on my knees, write the dedication to the little woman. Then I go on upstairs. The pale sun is shining again, the buses on Leibniz Street move with loud rumblings. Sounds and doors: and behind them Mrs. Borić, my parents, sisters, Marina in Meudon. She is dragging a heavy basket up to the second floor of the house on the Avenue Jeanne d'Arc. Years and simultaneous emptiness. Why, when we seek to escape what is alien, is that where we travel?

■ □ ■ □ ■

"To be Nowhere oh Nowhere, you my country,"
wrote František Halas.

I bought my first book of Tsvetayeva's poems many years ago in Zagreb and brought it to Berlin. Here I looked for everything I could find about her, all the Russian, German, Italian editions. After 1982 she possessed our apartment on Mommsen Street, her books lay over all the tables, chairs, shelves, her poems, prose, letters. I read and collected. Everything else followed of its own accord.

Marina dedicated her first book of poems, *The Evening Album,* to her radiant memory of Maria Bashkirtseff. Marina had read her diary as a young girl. "I love Maria Bashkirtseff madly, with mad pain. I lived two whole years in a state of longing for her. She is as alive for me as I am myself." Marina loved Ariadna Scriabin. Ariadna gave birth to a daughter two days before Marina's son Mur was born and sent her a knitted jacket for him to Všenory. Marina notes in her exercise book: "Now we are equal—she, in 1922 still a girl (sixteen), and I already as I am now. I have a son—she has a daughter. Age—that's all canceled out now." Adriana, also a poet, married the Jewish writer David Knut. During the Second World War she was in the French Resistance movement. She was killed in 1944 in a battle, when she stumbled upon an ambush. Neither woman survived to see the end of the war. " . . . Now we are equal. . . ."

From 1916 Marina read and loved Anna Akhmatova. She also met Osip Mandelstam at that time, and it was probably from him that she first received some of Akhmatova's poems to read. The two women saw each other only once, in 1940, in Moscow. Later Anna Akhmatova wrote:

> Tonight we pass with you, Marina,
> through midnight Moscow,
> and behind us go millions the same. . . .

In this love lies also the root of Marina's respect for Maya-kovsky, which later, in Paris, none of the émigrés could understand. Notably, after the murder of Gumilyov, Akhmatova's husband, rumors that she had committed suicide spread through Moscow. Mayakovsky publicly expressed his sorrow for Anna, whom he thought to be dead, and Marina devoted a poem to him on that occasion. ("I saw him then in Poets' Café as shaken as a wounded animal.")

The heart of the girl, the young woman, is fervent. The signs of love are rooms we enter without knocking. In one of these rooms sits Boris Pasternak, he is constantly by Marina's side, until her death. Her friend Olga Chernova, who visited Marina in Czechoslovakia, writes: "In the overgrown Smi-hov near Prague, in a little room in which there was not a single chair, nothing at all, we spent hours reciting Paster-nak's lines from his collection *My Sister, Life*. I shall never forget that penetration of a poet into the essence of the poetry of another." Marina loved Rilke. That was the life she lived somewhere else, in poetry. "A man is a table and a bed, there-fore there is no need for him to own them." The young woman had begun to hate objects, the burden of them, very early. What would remain were ink and paper. And a life in letters too, in which distance could be overcome with the rapid handwriting of dream. And the poverty that sticks to the fingers would be forgotten.

Sana or Koka, as we called her, was the wife of the poet Ljubiša Jocić from Belgrade. She was very young when I met her. They lived in a little house on the edge of the town. Although we had known each other only a short time, they took me into their house after I had an appendix operation. Koka and Ljuba lived modestly in one room. In it there were only pictures, books, and a bed—for me now. We had no money then even for cigarettes, and we would sit in a circle smoking one while Ljuba read or recited poems. We sat on the floor and freedom rang in the lines. That life with them warmed my heart, the shackles around it burst. And the memory of them remained for a long time, it did not alter at all, it was a space for living long after Ljuba's death and Koka's departure from Belgrade. Long after that year, 1959, when we were all still in that little house.

The girl Koka wrote to me in Zagreb that year:

> . . . In school textbooks they write about poets so "poeti-cally." One would think that it was nice to be a poet. In fact, they mislead people. It is dreadful to be a poet. And a man is a poet only because he has to be, not because it is fun. I write because I have to. But I can already see that it's terrible. I've been doing it for several years now, I see that it's awful. When will what I'm working on see the light of day, and afterward, when it does, there'll be something new. And again several years of waiting. And so on forever. And at the same time I shall have to go on being a civil servant earning a salary of 15,000. I shall have to live "truly as in a madhouse," not managing to write to my friends, not managing to rest, to pause.
>
> Ljuba has stopped writing. If he does not need to, it will be lucky for him. I'm not forcing him to work at litera-ture, if he does not have to. But I'm afraid that his silence is only temporary, and that one day he'll have to carry on again. His book *Hidden Worlds* lay around publishing houses for six years, accepted–not accepted, finally Prosveta has taken it, they wanted to bring it out this spring, delayed it until the autumn, and they've already told me that they are leaving it for spring 1961. The same

thing is in store for me, without a doubt. I'm still young, I've been so little published, and I'm not tired yet. And I, who love so many of Ljuba's things, especially "Arastrati" and this book which is supposed to be coming out, I want him to stop writing, at least for a time. That would be like watching someone dying suffer, or rather, watching someone being killed and wanting him dead as soon as possible so that we wouldn't have to watch. Irena, don't think that I'm insensitive to him. On the contrary. Anyone close to him who saw him suffering would want this, above all anyone who loves him as much as I do.

As for me, nothing hurts me yet. I write because I have to, because it's a game for me, a pleasure, I write out of curiosity. Even if my work doesn't get published. My only fear is that I shall not always be young, fresh, and indifferent to so-called success and failure. I still think of myself as a civil servant, and the poet in me is all that pleases me. Imagine, one day I'm at the office, and all of a sudden I remember that a poem of mine has just been published in a newspaper. That's terribly grand for a civil servant, you know. Virtually impossible. One day a pen pusher, the next day a poem in the paper. Really grand.

Probably when I become a poet, they'll say something rude about me as a poet. Because they're really rude to poets. I shall scream, is that impudent publisher still hanging on to my poems, keeping my collection in a drawer, while they're spending good money publishing rubbish? That's shocking. Good literature brings in money too. It just takes time. Haven't writers often been worth people's while? Hasn't Dostoyevsky or Shakespeare made more money for publishers than Jack the Ripper or *Madonna of the Sleeping Car?* Didn't the unhappy Branko Radičević in the end bring in ten times more income than his unhappy life cost? Hasn't he brought in enough to support ten poets who will never bring in a dinar, ten poets who will fail, who will never become poets? Our fathers made mankind so much money with books that we new children, both talented and untalented, could go on living off that money for ten years if it were not for the impudence of the publishers with their luxurious offices, supreme commands of advisers, and armies of pen pushers.

I am still small, but I know everything. My Cune taught me. He's had his tail cut off, because it was infected and he had a fever. Now he no longer has a fever. He's quite well, but he's pulled the stitches out of his tail and tomorrow he'll have to go back to the doctor's.

There's no summer here, dear Irena. Nothing but rain. Tropical winter weather. Damp, warm, sometimes a bit cold. I'm due for a summer holiday without a holiday. All our winter dreams have been destroyed by the summer reality. . . . I see the two of us in an ocean from the earth to the sky like two dissolving fish joined by the sounds of their voices like electronic music, playing ball with suns, and lying on pebbles like countless children's fingers and laughing as they run toward each other.

These lines are a failure as a text, but they have nonetheless captured something of my joy, of my desire to be cheerful and happy with you. With no office, and without watches, zebra crossings, traffic lights. . . .

Later young Koka left Belgrade, the little house, that life, Ljuba. She lived for a time on little money in Paris. She wrote to me, a book of her poems was published. Then she returned to Belgrade. I hear that she is now working for a publishing firm. We never saw each other again.

> Born of a father and mother
> And Hungarian literature in Budapest
> Before the war. What came later—
> I no longer remember.
> My head is abandoning me, because it hurts so much. . . .

Sarlota Lányi, 1940, a forgotten poet today.

In Paris Marina writes: "The daily routine, which lays my brain to waste."

This was a foreign city, housework, shopping, gray apartment complexes in the suburbs, fear, constant impoverishment. Her daughter Alya as an old woman described the life of the Efron family then in a letter to French friends:

> . . . Mother's immoderateness in a world of moderation made her feel that everyone she spoke to was shut up within certain boundaries, which she would quickly overcome; let us not forget that she was a great poet, while the rest of us (except my father who was in many ways similar in terms of his spirit, even if a spirit of a fundamentally different kind)—were at best readers. . . . Throughout her life only two men were equal to her: my father and Pasternak. What can be said about the daily routine? You probably still remember Czechoslovakia yourself, the little house on the edge of the village, its poverty, which was cheerful because it was young; we lived on Seryozha's grant and a few rare earnings and gifts. In France, for the first two years—while Mother was publishing a lot and while there was still a deceptive interest in her work—we didn't live badly, but later (materially) we lived worse and worse. It's only now, when the circumstances of my life are better again, although not easy in every respect, that I see what beggars we were. There is no other word for it. . . .

"A needle is fire, fabric is smoke" . . . that sentence is the epigraph to Elsa Morante's novel *Lies and Spells.* In December 1983 I read the following in the *Husum News:* "The Italian writer Alberto Moravia has asked for public, financial assistance for his colleague Elsa Morante who is seriously ill. The sixty-year-old Signora Morante, who became well known even beyond the frontiers of her homeland with her novels *La storia* and *Aracoeli,* is in a Rome hospital following an attempted suicide. Moravia, who had been married to Elsa Morante and separated from her for twenty-five years, described the condition of the patient in the Turin paper *La Stampa:* Her legs are paralyzed and she is only occasionally conscious. Her treatment costs in the region of a hundred million lire a year, and his books do not bring in even two-thirds of that sum. 'I think that a writer like Elsa Morante, who is so important to our culture, the greatest woman writer of our country, has the right to ask her country for help so that she may survive,' writes the seventy-year-old Moravia in his unusual appeal."

From the past into the future—only an illusion?

"The only meat we ate was horsemeat," continued Alya in her letter. "At the market we bought only the smallest potatoes, and the cheapest, leftover fruit. We ate eggs only at Easter, butter was only for Father (TB) and for Mur (a small child). There were never any sweets. Our clothes came from other people, our shoes from other people's feet. In the course of my whole life in France I had only two dresses: the first one was sewn for me by friends the year we came—the other by a friend in 1937, the year we returned to the USSR, I was twenty-four then. We mended and sewed a few things for Mother—she appeared in public, she had to look 'respectable.' Mother always got up early and however hard life sometimes made it, she would sit at her desk and write—she went to her desk every day like a worker to his machine. . . . During the second half of the day she would take us children for a walk. To the wood near Meudon, Bellevue, we walked for a long time through the Banlieue, sometimes reaching Sèvres, the Seine. . . . Contact with nature never disappointed Mother, nature refreshed her and had no 'upper limit' as we people did. She liked the south more than the north, the land more than the sea, pine needles, dry earth. She was as tireless in walking as in writing. . . ."

From Paris in 1902, the year of my mother's birth, Daniel de Monfreid wrote to his friend Paul Gauguin: "You live like a wild being in a glorious climate, in touch with the sea, that great cleanser. You will come here to our artificial life, you will be poisoned by our products and you will have to endure disgusting little Europe. . . ."

Marina fled from the city. She sat on the Atlantic shore writing letters. Her little son scampered all over her, Alya played in the sand. In her letters she scarcely ever wrote about her husband. But Sergei sometimes traveled with them on vacation. In the dark room with the blinds down, leaning against the wall, stands a sick man. He is silent. Was it like that? He dare not go on the beach, in the sun. And the family still feeds on the bread of friendship and the bread of hope. It is 1926. Marina is thirty-four years old. And she is writing her loveliest poems.

I see us in the endless brightness like seabirds, our feathers are stuck together with tar. I see in the rooms friends whom no one visits anymore. There are pictures hanging here, manuscripts live there, although virtually no sound penetrates inside anymore. Closed, luxurious graves, already under the earth. There exists an art of catacombs, it passes through the world under the ground.

"My soul is well brought up," writes Marina to Rilke, who is in Sierre. He is living in the Hotel Bellevue, his house in Muzot has just been renovated. He is translating Valéry and writes, on 9 June 1926, an elegy for Marina Tsvetayeva. Marina remembered the name of the hotel; in September of the same year she would move to the Paris suburb which was also called Bellevue. Some weeks later she was to move to Meudon, to the Avenue Jeanne d'Arc. Just around the corner, she would see a large orphanage, somewhat further along the Val de Fleury, where Rilke once lived, in Rodin's house. The edges of the wood, the same street corners, a common space called Meudon. There is therefore a geography of love in the year 1926. And a geography of poetry.

The names of that common land, meeting places of coincidence, the words of their destinies, were noted by Marina in her poem "New Year's Letter." The rhymes are connected by the threads of different places, letters, years. And the poem is a house through which we pass in order to discover what once was. For two people who could not see one another.

"That world, understand that: light". . .

Savoy too was for both of them a landscape of yearning. But had they actually met there, as they wanted, in some small town near the Swiss border, what would have happened? What would they have said to each other that November day, as it snowed? Sitting in a café? The man beside her would have said: You must go back to the sea. And the woman would have asked: Who is it who is waiting there— and not waiting? We know—responsibilities. Cooking, sewing, poverty, Marina would say. And the poet would have asked about the husband and she would have said that he had tuberculosis, that he could not earn any money. Then the poet would have said, take up your pen. And she would have replied, do you think that all that's left is ink and paper? Would he have accompanied her to the station later, as she did not want to get into a car? Would they have walked for long? He was already seriously ill, he was wary of love, of partings.

At the station the swirling eddies of their words borne away by the wind and their already indistinct outlines.

Savoy remained forever a landscape of yearning, and after Rilke's death Marina wrote: " . . . With him I lost Savoy— where I shall never go now; on 31 December it fell through the center of the earth, together with the Alps. . . ."

"New Year Letter" is a mirror of reality and art. It is full of traces like the shiny little stones of a mosaic. On 22 August 1926, Marina replies to Rilke's query about the Russian word for nest: " . . . In Russian it's *gnezdo,* singular (nothing rhymes with it!). The plural is *gnëzda* (the *ë* is soft in pro-nunciation, almost like an *o*); it rhymes with *zvëzdy*—stars. . . ." Rilke writes that on the envelope beside Marina's name there was printed a blue figure seven: "Seven, my blessed number." Marina replies: ". . . The week, in Old Russian—a seven-day—a Russian number! Oh, there are lots more: seven plagues—one remedy, much else. . . ."

She thinks of a window when she thinks of him, and for her his name does not rhyme with our time—it dates from earlier and later—that is, from always. Marina writes to him: "The mouth I have always felt as a world." From the dark apartment in the suburb of Bellevue she sends Rilke a postcard, the last he received, and later she writes to Pasternak: "I am glad, Boris, that the last word he heard from me was Bellevue." On 31 December 1926, she turns to the poet, who is already dead: "At midnight tonight, I will drink with you (you know how I clink glasses—ever so lightly!) . . . tomorrow is New Year's Day, Rainer. 1927. Seven is your favorite number. . . ."

She heard of Rilke's death in the course of that New Year's Eve. And that night she began her poem, a letter for him, and she wrote to Pasternak: "I did not feel the cruelty of the blow . . . what I felt you will see from the letter to him finished yesterday (the seventh day—his day) and begun on the 31st (the day I was told). . . ."

Rainer Maria Rilke was buried according to his own wish in a quiet valley of the Rhône, in the little cemetery of Rarogne. These places also entered into Marina's poem.

Because all that's left is ink and paper.

Letters and poetry—imagination of equal strength. There is evidence that Marina was happy only in her letters. They were her life.

They were the fabric from which her poetry also lived.

Two years later, toward the end of December 1929, Marina met the painter Natalya Goncharova.

Paris, a café, grayness behind the glass. Two women sit opposite one another for the first time. The bony, tall Goncharova, whom Marina was to love at once. Partly because of the name of Pushkin's wife. Marina would go to the studio and soon begin her first long text about painting. After all, there were paintings as well, Marina.

In that text which has never been translated from Russian, Pushkin's wife is always present too—the destinies of the three women intertwine—the Paris sun is present as well, all the colors of Natalya's paintings, her workshop: ". . . I saw the workshop for the first time in daylight. Then the corridor, one of those innumerable corridors of old Paris buildings—was a chasm. But the workshop—because of the heat—was a smeltery. The patience of glass under the insupportable sun. Glass under the uninterrupted blows of the sun. Glass every point of which was a nucleus. The sun baked, the glass glowed, the sun baked and melted. I remember the sweat that trickled and the sleeves of some friends who were sawing a board. My first Goncharova workshop—the unadulterated image of labor in the sweat of your brow. And beneath the first sun. In such heat it is impossible to eat (it's not worth drinking anything), impossible to sleep, talk, breathe. Only one thing is possible, and that can always be done, always must be done—it is possible to work. And it was not the glass that melted—but the brow. I remember, that first time, somewhere to one side, some kind of terrace which later disappeared. Beneath it the gables of the roofs—above it one of Goncharova's Paris paintings— vertically above one of her suns—and I beneath it. In my life I had never felt hotter—better. The terrace disappeared with the sun. To step onto it from the workshop now in memory is just as impossible as summoning that sun. With it we too shall return. . . .

Some children have the gift of amusing themselves and other children need to be amused. "Give me something to do, I'm bored." It's clear what will become of that child, because, to be amused, it wants only something from outside itself. Empty hands, the empty inner life of the consumer and squanderer, for whom someone like Goncharova is always only the deliverer of goods. Their hand—a cuttlefish, their inner being—an insatiable abyss. Their movement—that of a colossus and a cuttlefish. Goncharova's movements—those of a girl from the very heart of things: doing, inventing, creating. The movement of action. The movement of talent. (And of a blow!) . . .

■ □ ■ □ ■

"What remains: isolated texts awaiting history,"
says Heiner Mueller.

The child chewed pencils. At the bottom of the funnel, very far away, I see its round head. Sun is falling into the room, but the apathy is physical. The child comforts itself with cookies. Later it examines its altered handwriting in surprise. The freckled hand now feeds itself differently on mysterious hope, it draws signs more firmly and then pauses. Beside the paper lie cigarettes, ash. It does not miss the sweetness in its mouth—but still. . . .

By traveling to another country it is only parts of the body that have moved away, the spirit does not travel. There, in the homeland, people are sitting in dim light this year. They are wearing dark coats, thick scarves. Their shadows move restlessly over the walls. The fact that I have left permits me to glance backward. And that is often the only image I have. Here ghosts pass through the room—here is a graveyard.

What I would like to discover is Marina's entry into my life. It is as though the text were being written along a blood vessel which gleams. But it is weak, that trace of a dead woman whom we did not know. I strengthen her outline with other times, I carry her about like a little rag animal, firmly pressed to my breast, I carry her through these rooms here, today, in the light. I do not think of the power cuts.

Always in the evening, when the sun had set, fear used to reign in our children's room. It was only much later that

THE SILK, THE SHEARS and MARINA; OR, ABOUT BIOGRAPHY

Marina grew fearful. The child-tree practiced immediately, very early, anticipation and defense. But, in the end, that was not much use either. We were just afraid in different ways.

But sometimes the tracks are very deep, brilliant. Large suit-cases, bags of bread stand on the wooden floor, on the worn boards. That is the luggage of time. There as here. She is standing beside shoes, old baskets, unread books. She stands in various towns and slowly grows into a dark, unrecogniz-able heap. All that is written touches her in passing, like a brief backward glance.

Marina knew the feelings of parting. She traveled through Europe and stood before the closed windows of a foreign land. What distinguished her was the strength of her own language. The woman, a poet, stands in a faded dress. In var-ious dwelling places which no longer exist. But the luggage is common to everyone, and it remains. Despite the time which passes. I love Marina irrationally.

"Marina no longer drags her rare visitors toward the Všenory horizon, she sits at her table wrapped in all the shawls she possesses, knitting (the madness continues—a child?) or writing," writes her husband Sergei in a letter.

When I wake up, in Berlin, I do not see any kind of horizon. Only a gray window. And I always mutter, that isn't any-thing. Everything is as it always was. Even today nothing points to any kind of misfortune. Misfortune? The clock was not wound on purpose. There's no hurry, have a good rest. Not to hear the clock, the telephone. To be free. Free? The curtains are gray too. In the pillow there's still a foolish dream about a river in which white rabbits swim and shout. Then it's better, as always, to get up. Grayness.
After ten minutes I close the window in alarm. There's fog outside, poison. The stench will remain in the room like a

skin. I have trouble breathing. Will they give the smog warning today? No fresh air whatever enters this room. Down below, in the courtyard, after the trash bins have been emptied, there is silence. Silence. Poison. The window panes are clouded, I ought to clean the windows. I ought to.

In the kitchen I make coffee. I wash the lime scale out of the pan. The gas makes a noise, the water makes a noise. There is a fine crust of washing powder on my dressing gown. A smell or my imagination. In the newspaper I read a speech by the writer Frisch. Where does he live and where do I live? Why we are in the same world, with the same loud newspaper headlines? My powerlessness marvels at him. Perhaps it isn't all like that. What do I mean: like that? I lean on the chair and try to think about hope. I know, all of it is deliberate, all that bad news with which the newspapers here want to hold you in their fists. It's not real, all these feelings of fear. It's nothing, nothing, it's possible to get up.

My coffee is cold. Through the kitchen pass traveling actors from Angelopoulos's film. They walk across the boards. As always, so also here. No one fires anymore, but we are dead. That is good. I get up and go into the room: dead. Behind me moves a whole host of actors, they sit down with me on the chairs, on the blue cushions. Pathetic, always worn out, the future.

The flat corridor is nicely dark and cold. The dust reminds me that everything will be left undone, if I do not once and for all force myself to accept the day, if I do not finally wake up. It's all just a game, my dear, it must not be allowed. You'll work. Who can spend the whole day in a dressing gown? I could not if I had children. But why do I not have children? Not, I suppose, for the sake of such freedom?

Under my hands a wall, quite smooth. Everything is hermetically sealed, as though it were all in a plastic bag. Tied up and soundless. I take three steps—and remember my mother. My mother from Vienna who came to Belgrade and then went to Zagreb. I see her in her room rushing to and fro.

Old, dependent, helpless. And it is too late for anything. The polish of the furniture has become dull. Only the china tinkles in the glass cabinet and awakens memories of tables laid for celebrations. There is nothing anymore. I know that it seems that way to Mother and memory is imprisoned in her as is unhappiness.

I must endure that falling down the stairs of my childhood with its "küss die hand" and its pink ribbons in the hair. Oh good stair end, where everything is broken. Later I learned that we do not belong anywhere if we remain in the cave. We have described the pillars of blood and pain wrongly, we did not understand anything and so we destroyed everything. We could not, because we carry in ourselves an unbridgeable fear in the face of physical suffering. We complain for a long time with the help of words. Shut in our rooms, our houses, we cannot touch what we would like to. The earth, plowed fields, plants. I stretch out my hand to my mother and console her with false comfort. She has remained a foreigner in the southern land where she lives. The lovely warm light does not penetrate into her room. She often wrote, I can't, I won't. In the bathroom I decide to wash the clothes in cold water. My back over the bath takes on that real painful arch, I scratch the stain under the tap with my nail. Then, in the whiteness that appears, I see the field I once ran through.

"I live a domestic life, I like it and I can't get used to it—it's like a place midway between the cradle and the grave—but I was never a child, never a dead person," says Marina.

The washing drips. Now I ought to go shopping. How do you say: A loaf of bread, please? How do the heavy doors open and close? Without thinking, I button and unbutton my coat. There is little I can endure. How to escape from the glass house where I have been shut up because it's nice to have children. Mother thinks it was by chance; Father is dead, I can't ask him.

I stand in my coat in front of the door. The key in my hand has grown warm already and that means that I possess an apartment. Also a glass house? When I began to ask that I already had so many things that I could no longer free myself from them. For a long time it seemed normal to have an apartment, an address, to register with the police as a foreigner, to have a residence permit. A passport, a name, a family. What does this longing for movement mean now? Without a passport I can't go anywhere anyway. Wherever I look, I see orderly freedom. Everything here lives within a huge space with fences, walls. Within it we play at movement. I know, one shouldn't think about that, I must lock the door of the apartment, I must protect the unnecessary. I must be afraid of burglars, I must not scream. Everything is all right. Be humble, it will be worse. You will be amazed. Yes, good. I don't care.

I tell Mother that I don't care which dress I wear—I'm going to the cinema—and she never forgives me.

Old fabrics, faded blouses, discarded shoes, skirts, hats, photographs, a torn dress of washed-out silk, a small muff, a little fur coat from Slovenia, bottles of cod-liver oil, socks that slipped down, handkerchiefs—all that: a gown of memories. When I look at it now I become completely calm and I put it away in the wooden trunk, I close it. No more descriptions, no more yearning.

In France, after they had left Všenory near Prague, Marina said: "Czechoslovakia simply no longer exists. I have transformed it into a buried manuscript."
In Orwell's year everyone practices forgetting languages. And feelings are called: retreat. Only documents rule. A knot of feelings—is that merely a cocoon from a bourgeois world? We are altered when the trembling sound reaches us. Yes, of course. And yet, speech still flows in tiny currents, lies like a sample on the paper.

Marina stopped writing in 1939. Dora stopped speaking in 1978.

Tsvetayeva crosses the Arbat and surrounding streets in long strides, her body resists the wind, writes a friend. Always against the wind. In 1918 she was alone in Moscow; the young woman felt bitterly that many people no longer needed what she cared for. Books, romanticism, the world of one's forebears, old verses. And she herself felt superfluous, no one asked about her, the general suspicion offended her. That is how a person slips out of the routine. Her decision to leave Moscow was the decision of a hurt woman, for whom nothing was left but to search for her husband. That was her legendary stubbornness. So this departure really made an émigré of the poet, who in every poet saw an émigré without a country. That is how one comes to a place one never wanted to reach. For in Paris, among the expatriate nobility, among the wealthy, she was quickly revealed as a foreigner, as someone who did not belong among the "better" people. And everything she did was suspect: She wrote, she smoked, she loved, she was poor, and she hated their blind political hatred of everything that came from the homeland. Like a person who wanted only one thing: to write, she fell through the sieve of those better circles, was left alone in Paris as well, felt herself superfluous. Those people quickly and coldly refused to offer her their hand.

We had already emerged from an erosion—of family, of society. The ignorance of our fathers was frightening and we wanted to leave our home as quickly as possible. I gathered, and built myself of, scattered thoughts, vague feelings. I examined carefully, like a watchmaker, every separate little piece from which I had been patched together. Out of the silent world of three-room apartments we fled into cellars, into chasms, deliberately.

This summer in Zagreb, I find a dark exercise book with

graph paper in a drawer. In 1926 my mother began to write a diary. She was twenty-four and she longed for unknown happiness. She would never see the sea like that in Saint-Gilles. She was forever weeping.

In September 1940 Marina writes in her diary:

> About myself. Everyone thinks I'm brave. But I don't know anyone who is more fearful. Everything frightens me. An eye, blackness, footsteps, but most of all myself, my head—it is my head that serves me so faithfully in my exercise books but kills me in life. No one sees, no one knows that for years already I have been searching for a large hook; but there isn't one, there's electricity every-where, no chandeliers.—I've been trying out death for years already. Everything is ugly and terrible. To swallow something—nausea. To jump—hostility. Water—arche-typal fear. I don't want to be confused after my death, but it seems I already fear myself—after my death. I don't want to die, I want not to be. Foolishness. As long as someone still needs me . . . but God, how small I am, how little I know. To go on living—to go on chewing. Bitter gall. . . .

Women's emotions, emotions of the time? These are war years. One person cannot come to terms with himself, another cannot come to terms with his work. Two reasons for life, for death. For one person, apathy on the surface, for another—weariness in her inner being.

When night-candles bloom, on the terrace in Zagreb, they bloom for two nights. They are flowers from embankments, deserted places. Here in Berlin I saw them only once, between the overgrown lines at the former railway station of Gleisdreieck. They came to Europe from America as early as 1614 and they always remind me of the edge of the city near Meudon. They flower bright yellow every year, they don't need tending. The petals fade quickly, they have something of the quality of sensitive skin, a transient charm, as they remind one of abandoned places which are already completely overgrown.

Marina loved the red berries of the rowan, the tree that grows beside country paths. The first flowers of the juniper which I loved were full of earwigs. Juniper grew in the station of the little village in Slovenia. I never touched its petals again. My mother was frightened too, she forbade me to. Since then at night, earwigs have crawled into my ears in my dreams. That's how flowers are taken away from children and the pleasure of touch is lost. The realm of trees, leaves, and grass remained unexplored for a long time. Gardens were just a terrible jungle for me. The awkward child-tree scampered cautiously between the bushes. Dark stains lay on the meadows of childhood and in them were ants, lizards, terrible beetles. A town child, thought the villagers.

But I was not that either. Later I found a book about butterflies among my father's books. And so I searched, through pictures, for a way back to that meadow.

In Meudon Marina picked forget-me-nots and watched her husband. Because Sergei wanted only one thing: to go back to Russia. Alya wanted that too, that was the beginning of the first misunderstandings with her mother. Did Sergei do something wrong in 1937 in order to "earn" his return? Rumors about his spying activities spread through Paris. Marina and Alya never believed them. Was Sergei the victim of anti-Semitic circles in Paris then? Did they hate him also because he wanted to go back? Hatred toward Marina as well therefore, because of her pride and defiance? Was Sergei a broken, sick man already, before 1937, before he was shot in 1941? No one can answer those questions now. That much justice, at least, should be left for someone who cannot defend himself.

His grave in the darkness of time.

The father and the daughter Alya returned first. Alya too was arrested in 1939. Later, from 1948 to 1954, she lived in exile in Turhansko in the north. She no longer had anyone. She did have one friend of Marina's left, he wrote to her, sent her books: Boris Pasternak. All those years in endless cold and dark had destroyed Alya's health. In 1955, for want of any kind of guilt, she was rehabilitated. After that she lived in Moscow collecting and publishing her mother's works, searching for all the manuscripts she could find, and in 1975 she died of a heart attack on the street. Marina's sister, who was also exiled (the sister with whom she had recited poems in duet and with whom she lost touch when she left Russia), was also rehabilitated; she still lives in Moscow, and is writing Marina's memoirs.

The girl Alya, the young woman, life in solitude. No real life at all, only a path of sacrifice.

Marina's daughter. In the winter of 1921 Marina and Alya had a visitor in Moscow. The visitor was amazed at Marina's crystal-and-bronze inkwell: such a charming piece and—so dirty. Marina replied: "Everything of mine is dirty." And Alya said: "Everything except your soul." Alya was ten years old then. And in December 1918 she wrote in her diary: "My mother is very strange. . . . She is sad, quick, and loves Poems and Music. She writes poems. She is patient and tolerant in the extreme. Even when she's angry she is loving. She is always in a hurry. She has a big heart. A gentle voice. A quick step. Her fingers are full of rings. Marina reads at night. . . ."

The real tree of my childhood was not drawn. It was the big lime tree in the little park above Bosanska Street. I used to run to it when there was a storm in our house, when my sisters were crying, when the telephone was ringing, the maid shouting, my parents running through the rooms. Then I used to creep out of the apartment, run off to the hill and sit under the tree. I would sit helplessly, without knowing why.

That lime is still there. It has grown still taller and more luxuriant, the benches in the park have become worn. Today
other children come and sit under that tree. They do not
want to be seen, they throw stones if I get too close to them.
Those children no longer cry, there are many of them.
Changes brought by time. For the secret of the tree has been
uncovered, people are writing about its imminent death. For
me it was still eternal and the miracle of a roof over my head.

Forget me, I say to the friends who are abandoning me.
What is happening to Marina and to me is a present without
reason. Security under trees.

A drunken man chased me, shouting through the empty
stairway of the old radio station. Trembling, I locked myself
in an office, waited for darkness to fall, and then crept home.
Later the man became one of the directors of the radio station and he thought I had a hold on him. He tried to harm
me whenever he could. Then he forgot everything. Includ-
ing me. Yes, a terrible love and a terrible hatred. Or, as he
put it, "passion." But actually he was just aroused by a good
little bourgeois girl. Years, economics, change everything.
Today he has gray hair and is very well dressed. And he walks
up the steps without looking at anything.

Wartime here, friendships do not live long. At home in
Zagreb our neighbor tells me about her sick husband: Now
he is as light as a butterfly, he hovers around the apartment,
touching everything tenderly. In the evening, on the terrace,
we sat drinking wine from the island of Hvar, a friend said:
He is with us now, the dead painter, I know that for sure. Fill
up another glass, please! Urban oblivion is stronger than the
forgetfulness of peasants. It is not good that I have become a
traveler.
Marina lost her readers when she left Russia. In her one good
dress she would hold literary evenings during her first years in

Paris. That was in various small, stuffy rooms and for Russian émigrés. Not a single French person ever came. There would be one table and one chair at the front of the room. The people who listened sat on benches. Ever fewer people. The poems were pungent, glowing, unclear. Some people just whispered about her hair being too short, about her impoverished appearance. And about whether she had another lover again. But, despite everything, she read unwaveringly on. The miserable fee was paid to her in public, in front of everyone. There was never any discussion after the reading, people left the room in silence. But Marina would always keep on trying to read her poems somewhere. Right up until 1937, then they stopped inviting her. They forgot Marina.

A friend, a Chilean who lives in Berlin as a political émigré, read some of his fiction the other day in the Einstein Club. There was a large table with wine, fruit juice, glasses, in an anteroom. In another room there was a table with a chair for him. And emptiness. His German colleagues did not come. There were only five of us, and that was "close family," as we call it. Not a single unknown listener or lover of literature. Literary evenings in a foreign country. The fee of one hundred marks is not paid in public. The organizer asks us for his account number. As our friend has no account, there is a confused bustle. What should be done? In the end they decide to send me the fee and then I can give it to him. The wine was undrunk, the glasses untouched. Only bright light, a loud emptiness. I see Marina sitting beside us, her eyes are closed. Then the question of belonging to literary circles was a question of political conviction, here it is a question of the market and a name. Later, on the rainy street, we laughed out loud and went to a Greek restaurant.

The curtains of time fall over the places which we ought to avoid in the future. There are no surprises left. The program goes on according to an exact plan and without deviation.

And the dream about the poem takes up even less space than it did then in Paris.

Marina's pen scratched across the paper every morning. It was a matter of art. The poem, proclaimed dead so often already, does not want to die. For apart from danger in the world, there exists also longing for the morning reality. That should not be forgotten. If a person is alive, then he seeks that other kind of bread as well.

Dora will never again stand on a stage. She's in a clinic in Zagreb. I talked to her doctor this summer. He doesn't have much hope. Nothing touches her anymore, he said. It is as though she were frozen, we can no longer reach her. That is what she wants. Medicine cannot help now. The whole success of the treatment lies in the fact that Dora has begun to knit a scarf. Awakening, she is once again "taking part" in life. The admission of powerlessness over the world which had turned Dora into a stone arouses pity for the doctor. And in any case he believes in another art of treatment. On his desk lie books of poems, he writes to writers, talks to them. His room is dark, outside is heavy, searing heat. Someone shouts through the barred window, looking for cigarettes. I see only his outstretched hand. In the night, before they brought her to the clinic, Dora sat in her kitchen holding a knife in her hand. She sat like that until five o'clock, then the knife fell out of her hand. When I parted from Z., I made my first film with the young actress Dora. She came to the studio in a white blouse and dark skirt. That was in 1961. Dora was cheerful and full of faith in art. The spotlights did not spoil her naturalness. Later the difference between the work of acting and that faith became ever greater and her strength began to wane. When we met later, she used to talk absently about the deadly rehearsals. And about fear. Then she lay down in her bed and forgot everything. We didn't see Dora that summer. Her room is somewhere above an avenue of chestnut trees. A scarf. Something so slight is what we call hope. The dream of art is also always the one that is against functioning. Perhaps that dream will flash once more, course through her fingers, in the woolen strands of the scarf as they are knitted. But that is a different kind of light. It will be woven into the scarf and extinguished there.

Marina and Mur are sitting on a train. The journey in the summer of 1941 to Yelabuga. Moscow is being evacuated, the train is full of refugees. The rope tied around the suit-case was given to Marina by Pasternak. He would wonder later whether it was he who had provided her with the rope she needed. They are not carrying much with them. Some sugar, grain, rice. A few silver spoons to sell or exchange. In her bag is an exercise book in which she no longer writes poems. And tobacco for cigarettes. She is silent, the plains pass before her eyes. Mur watches her with resentment. He resents their profound poverty, and the fact that they are so badly dressed. She listens to the boy who is sixteen years old. What can she reply in her weariness? She is thin, silent. They eat their last piece of bread. Mur forces from her a promise to buy him a new suit.

They stand for a long time at some station, then in the har-bor at Yelabuga. She does not know where to find a room. The town is overflowing with refugees. They only have money for a few days. Had Mur not been with her, Marina would have lain down on the ground and never moved again.

My mother exchanges a ring for a loaf of bread. That was during the flight to Zagreb, in 1941. We are traveling in a crowded train, children are shouting, women weeping. What is repeated are pictures. But not the content.

The child was told to shut the windows and doors. No, in Zagreb no alarm signal was given. The child was told it was because of the neighbors. They did not have to hear the child crying and shouting. Then the father brought the yellow stick. The child would be beaten, it would be punished. It no longer knew for what misdeed. War and new dangers did not alter the father's educational methods. His blows are hard. The stubborn child does not cry. And the father, dissatisfied, stops hitting it. Get out of my sight! Where to? The child doesn't have a room of its own, it sleeps in the living room. Outside it's evening already, the child no longer dares go out into the street, doesn't dare go to the tree. Thinking of all of that, the child forgets its pain. It forgets everything, but not that it had obediently to close the doors and windows, before the "punishment." That was what made it most helpless. Stupid wretch, go away! The father shouted. And the child went quietly out of the apartment, out of the family's life, by night, and in a dream.

I would like to enter into every little piece of the dark wood. When someone shouts I think of Father.

And of the dress of memories. I think of my fellow travelers. Of Koka, of Branko. I think of Ivan Picelj in the silence of his white room assiduously painting his tranquil geometric forms. I think of Marijana S. in Berlin, an unknown painter of these loud times. Marijana S. Sometimes I think it is good, if a little is still left in the dark, in a small apartment, on a Berlin street whose name—Akazienstrasse—reminds me of the white treetops of my homeland. Sometimes it seems like that to me. For in art there is a loudness which quickly comes to mean a siege. And that is no longer happiness.

There has been enough unhappiness. After a happy childhood in Lika and Zagreb. She came to Germany as a young woman in 1965, with a husband who was always a stranger to her. She lived at first in Schwarzwald, there she began to paint. To get over her anxiety, as she told me. Then partings, loss, illness, a foreign land. And always painting. By night, by day, in little kitchens, in small bedrooms. Paintings like a gathering of time. Unforgetting. Everything that life surrounds finds its place on the canvas: worn-out dresses, letters, photographs, the dry stem of a rose. All the rejected things of a woman's life.

Since 1979 Marijana S. has been living in Berlin. I met her late, by chance, at the opening of her exhibition in Wedding. Since then I go into the empire of the women's tales which she paints, writes, tells. I am not much concerned about cataloging this work. Its expression is: truth, dream, instinct. The chances of this not being noticed in this large city are very great. Let it be so. That is how she lives, breathes. When I sit in the kitchen in Akazienstrasse I can converse with paintings. I get to know the shape of someone's life, sensitivity, out of time.

Let it be so. My conversations with my fellow travelers are secret.

The dress of memories reaches to our feet, Marina. Is it a child's dress? And that which happened yesterday? Is it still so close that it is shaped as though we were looking at it through a magnifying glass? Time, which has not yet become a body, evaporates very easily.

I should like to enter into every little piece of the blueness. There is the sea and that woman writing.

■ □ ■ □ ■

" . . . Myth knows no shroud, all are alive, all go
into death alive, some with a branch, some with
a book, some with a toy . . . ," writes Marina.

Which picture will be the last? A part of the sky, a wall, the
smooth whiteness of a hospital room? The edge of a bed, the
pattern of a rug, a high ceiling? Will we be lonely, old, forgotten? Or will the pain of the last moment come suddenly,
as it did by the gray pedestrian island where Angel, an irre-
placeable friend, fell, fatally injured by the mirror of a
cement-mixer truck, that 28 December 1983? And the streetcar he was waiting for never arrived. His last sight was perhaps the tall gray building opposite, with the balcony on
which we had been together that summer, he, Sanda, their
sons. Death came from behind, armed with the iron around
the mirror, a machine of war in the middle of the city for
someone standing, and waiting. For someone who was gentle, wise, his eyes filled to the brim with the forgotten landscapes of a childhood in Kumanovo. Angel. Without a word,
surprised. And the pain in us does not pass, will not pass. A
body lies in the street and everything is the past. Splinters of
glass all around. When we were together for the last time, one
evening, at his and Sanda's flat, a bulb above the table had
shattered and we were afraid, scattered with silver splinters. A
mirror broke half a year later, everything was cold, everything
gray. The threads were cut, words half spoken, warmth unattainable. The town which is far from here lies in my memory
like a black clod. I know how those close to him are grieving
now, and everyone in that room at the Zagreb television stu-

dios where we worked together for so many years. I see them standing in front of the big desk with photographs under heavy glass. And that room has never changed, it received me as a familiar friend for years later, in that room you did not know what forgetting was. I first saw Angel in 1948, also at a streetcar stop. The one by the theater. I was on my way to school, he was a student, I remembered his face, it was different from the others. When we met we were young and we loved film. Then we worked together in television. For ten years, with Sanda, Zora, Vicko, Dijana, Ivan. And we lived communally. Angel did not buy a car, the old furniture was carried into the new apartment that had the balcony, and books, books, a painting by Murtić. Ten years, twenty. His sons grew, some friends left the town, new ones came, and Angel's room at the studios was unchanged, it was always the place for people to meet. Suddenly now everything is left unsaid, and the room empty. Only in our memory do we touch the places of our lives. Zagreb, Pula, Dubrovnik, streets in these towns. Pain, destiny, torment. I stare into the moment of the accident. Just one step further forward, or had the streetcar arrived earlier, or had the driver not been driving like that, why, how? The height of the mirror, the height of a man. Here in Berlin I run through the town, looking at all the car mirrors, measuring, grieving, I run on. Where does that black curtain come from, and the last image? Snow keeps on falling. We know the smile, the look, we hear the voice, we see images. We still feel the hoop of pain on our skin left by that day in December. And the glare of finality. Therefore not silence, on no account. We must speak, think, take you everywhere with us, ask you questions, listen. To ensure your place, say your name. We must live unforgetting. And so accept the loss. I telephone Zagreb, I hear Sanda's voice, far away.

The last image is silent.

We get up, we walk, we talk. And beside us, emptiness. Always. Notes with black edges lie in the drawer with letters and photographs. What is it we are keeping here? Out of what depths do we pull the kerchief of forgetfulness or unforgetting? A graveyard in the apartment, in our heads.

The last image. In Yelabuga Marina saw—or else she had shut her eyelids tight—a little piece of faded wallpaper. No light came into the room from the window. In the kitchen, in an iron pan there were cold, fried fish left over from the previous evening. Her son Mur had gone with the landlady to work at the airfield. It was 31 August 1941.

Why do I see that day in snow as well? It was summer. Perhaps it was hot. Birds were singing, flowers were blooming in the garden. And the cold was inside. At the moment of Marina's death, in Moscow Ehrenburg's wife dropped a bracelet on the pavement and it broke. A bracelet that Marina had given her.

That had been in the Crimea. They were all there, all still young men and women. They were sitting on the wooden veranda or in the garden. It was in Koktebel, in the poet Max Voloshin's house, where Marina's fateful journey began. Among Max's guests in 1911 she fell in love with Sergei Efron.

Voloshin was one of the first to recognize Marina's talent. He wrote a review of her book *The Evening Album,* and looked for her in order to give her the review in person. Marina thanked him for the review in a letter: "You treat the book as you do life and you forgive life what is not forgiven literature."

After that she went often to Koktebel to the Voloshinovs. That was where she saw Osip Mandelstam for the first time. Three of his poems from the volume *Tristia* are dedicated to her.

> I do not seek her, Cassandra, the seconds blossomed:
> it was not your eye I sought, I did not seek your lips.
> But now in December—oh solemn Vigil—memories
>   torment us. . . .

MARINA; OR, ABOUT BIOGRAPHY

Natalia Rubenstein, a former worker at the Pushkin Museum, used often to visit Voloshin's widow, Maria Stepanova, in the seventies. The house was still standing, an old, dilapidated house, with the shadows of all those who once stayed in it. Today the upper part of the house contains Voloshin's collection, his paintings, books, letters. The downstairs rooms are used by the Soviet Union of Writers as a rest home. Natalia Rubenstein writes: "At Christmas Maria Stepanova lights candles in the house. For all those who once visited her house and who are now dead. One candle for Marina, one for Seryozha Efron, for Marshak, Bulgakov, and for . . . many, many candles. And every year there are more of them."

"I am used to being alone," says Maria Stepanova. "There was an outbreak of cholera, you know what that means. Sometimes a person has to pay what's due. You can't simply take, grab, earn, plunder the land. Never giving anything away, never saving, not reflecting about anything. Never repaying your debts to nature and not thinking of punishment. People would prefer to forget the very word. . . ."

There were always rooms in which people sat and read poems, talked about literature. They were small rooms, on the ground floor, rooms in little guesthouses at the sea, in places of one's childhood. Now they lie in a row like a youthful ribbon of hope. Their light, cigarette smoke, voices are preserved in memory. The future was anticipated; war was waged against cowardice—against illness, enemies—against death. People laughed, cried, loved. Poems were written at night, after work, sometimes on the streetcar, on one's knees in the doctor's waiting room. On Sundays, when the empty summer roads lay like white veins around the dark rooms, in the quivering mornings, in holiday homes, always, even without a trembling manuscript. The days of icebergs, work, loud measurability had not yet come, shadows were sought for art and not the loud light of the stage. Desires had not yet changed into what was nearest: into fame, cars, fear. These rooms no longer serve as meeting places, the hands of large clocks devour time like swift-legged beetles. And whatever wishes to stop will be crushed. Biographies are increasingly like fairy tales, sleep is assured and therefore lost. Now the luxury of brilliance speaks, say the mad, beggars, prophets. What we really are, for time, is tedious baggage.

In the end Marina and Mur took a boat ride on the River Kama. Like many writers they did not have a permit to move into Chistopol, they had to come to overcrowded Yelabuga. Marina found just one day's work there. She washed dishes in a cafeteria. Cold in the month of August, the war which was moving closer, her awkwardness—what was the reason for her terrible decision? The rope was firm, her strength spent. The girl in her died that morning, she fell into the deep well of time, she sank, grew old.

But the cornelian from the Crimea survived everything. It was found later, among her dead daughter's things.

The room in Yelabuga was divided in half by a curtain. On the right was Marina's bed, on the left a couch for Mur. "I shall stay here, I'm not going any further," said Marina in that room.

At first the landlady did not like her. "She was dreadfully thin," she said, "bent, gray as a widow. She wore a gray cap on her head. We got a bit closer through her smoking. She didn't know how to roll cigarettes. She lived with us for ten days with her son Mur. She was depressive, silent, she smoked. When she washed her hair she tired herself so much that she wasn't able to wipe the floor."

The landlady did not criticize Marina for her suicide, but said that Marina had killed herself too soon, that she still had plenty of food. "When I came home on Sunday I knocked into the chair and saw her hanging. I did not dare touch her body. She had left several notes behind her. That was good because of the police. The doctor and police came two hours later. She still had a little money, four hundred rubles. A loaf of bread cost a hundred and forty. She left two letters as well. Only the son and the police read the letters. The son left on 4 September 1941, the day after the burial. He went to Tashkent, where he lived in great poverty. He joined the army as a volunteer. He took sugar, rice, and grain with him. As soon as they had taken his mother away, he began to iron his suit and get dressed up. He spent only two days in the room, he did not sleep there. He fell in the war, he was sixteen years old."

"If I had known she was a poet, I would have gone to the funeral," the landlady also said. As it is, no one knows where her grave is.

Mur was young, he accused his mother of being incapable, impractical. And she was a woman without her husband, without her daughter or sister. Nothing could warm her any longer. Her life had passed swiftly, in a instant. In the deep pocket of her apron there were no longer any exercise books filled with poems. That current had left her body and into it, instead of imagination, had come a deathly weariness.

August 1941: the last Jews of the town of Zagreb are sent away to camp. On 31 August at home we celebrate my mother's birthday. I remember a long taffeta dress, white skin. What was going on outside was unknown to her. I found out about it all at fourteen, after the war.

We live and carry on. And read the Book of the Dead. I saw Dora more rarely. While we were making films together, for her, a student of the Theater Academy, the past played no kind of role, she did not talk much about herself, she recited her poems in the studio and then rushed straight off to her speech exercises. When we saw each other again she was already married. I often came to Zagreb. She would smoke all night, no one told me that. Then the absence in her eyes became complete. When she came into a room, she would say only, I'm fine, I'm fine. And the more she retreated the more she anchored herself in me, became the embodiment of my guilt. The guilt of not looking, not touching, of our lives just side by side. Dora, a person whom we lost: Time proclaimed her sick. I carry in me the fact that I cannot penetrate through the dark door of her resistance like some lost hope of youth. And now it is too late, I can no longer go to her.

For assistance I often invoked a degree of unreason, safe shores, a sense of reality. I wanted to live. I did not get lost, I always found my way around in my half-sleep, in loss and consolation.

To write is also to name the guilt. But you cannot forgive, Dora, you do not have to.

When someone goes off into the unknown, then we have all failed too. Many people then say, that is destiny.
I want to find them, all traces in the realm of silence and the night.

An examination of the memory seems sometimes to be divided from the body. My lips carefully follow the biography in a strange remoteness from me. And the body just slowly warms up, stepping once again through all that once was, through helplessness, through hope. And then swiftly moves away.

The body hovers above the landscape like that child which Stančić painted, like that dream of Marina's. The title of the painting: childhood. But the painter in Zagreb, whose heavy body had grown weightless through illness, put out the light in their quiet kitchen in 1977 forever. We sat in that kitchen for many years, the white tiles gleamed, on the table were fruit and cakes.

Once, many years before Stančić's death, he had written on a scrap of paper: "I'm going into the kitchen to eat sugar. It's Friday, eleven P.M., no one is considerate, no one is wearing themselves out for me. But still: I shan't be able to sleep now. I shall walk through empty Gaj Street to the Square. As though I were going somewhere, to look at something—in some shop window—life is still here. Be a friend."

He has been dead for eight years now, the studio is empty, the kitchen dark, unrecognizable to me, unreachable. Gaj Street is empty, the sugar has been spilt. The child is somewhere far away, on some other star.

The people I love are immortal, said Alya Efron.

Sand flies into the eyes. That is a comfort for those who are left. The pine cones burst open loudly and from that moment their scent has been merged with an intimation of the end.

What is left is to draw another geographical map of memory.

Marina Tsvetayeva was born on 9 October 1892 in Moscow. Her father was a teacher and director of a museum, and that in prerevolutionary Russia meant: a house with a garden, rooms with books, a piano. A nanny with whom folktales also came into the house. It meant knowledge of at least two foreign languages, education abroad. Openness to everything new and love of tradition. But the chronicle of the Tsvetayev family shows cracks, its frame is not only bourgeois life. Marina's father's first wife was the daughter of the historian Ilovaisky. Marina had a half sister and a half brother.

Early conflicts, cruel death in the Ilovaisky family were warnings which early aroused in Marina suspicion of so-called harmony, early determined her step. Her parents did not send her to an elegant school, but to a Catholic institute in Lausanne and Freiburg. That was where she began to write verse in German and French. That was in 1906, the year her mother died. "I regret only the sun and music." Marina was later to write: "After such a mother there was only one thing left for me, to become a poet." That strange mother, obsessed with love of music, days with her sister Asya in their summer house in Tarusa, the Oka River, red rowans by the roads, that blue island of childhood, all these will be found again in her first poems. Loss, death, time. The irresistible birth of happiness. Growing up. As a mature woman Marina writes to her friend Ana Teskova in Prague: "I was left angular (like all who grow up without mothers). But more inside. And I was left an orphan."

In my sleep the house of my Zagreb childhood stands in Berlin. Everything is still in it, the furniture, the Sirovy paintings, family friends. There is no dust anywhere, although by now the house has been empty for forty years. I pass through the rooms in surprise, I am glad to have found it again. I look at a painting by Sirovy once again. And I am afraid, I see that I was mistaken. It is not that picture but some pale, badly drawn landscape. I was mistaken, the house no longer exists. This is a strange house, with strange things. I can no longer reconstruct that old one. That fear and that happiness. That's how it seems in my dream.

Between 1910 and 1928, during Marina's lifetime, nine volumes of her verse appeared, two long poems and a dramatic sketch. All the rest—essays, prose, letters, and poems written abroad—appeared only scattered through Russian journals in Paris. In Russia people were already suspicious of her, as they were later of her grave. Only after Stalin's death did there begin a new "discovery" of the poet, in Moscow in 1962, 1965, and 1967 her first books appeared. And people are reading them again.

> For my poems, as for good wine,
> the time will come, for sure.

Times of traveling. Attempts at life in different places. It is often said, we choose what is foreign. But then the years change everything. I am no longer a true witness, that is a reproach. For some, what I say is still only a text. But distance is not only distance, there is presence even without a shared place. Or do changes lie perhaps outside the borders we cross with road maps? Partings are ever more frequent. Then a person loves what is lost.

In the suitcase are dreams, books. A journey circling a round hill made of the rags of life. Within a territory through which we pass without a passport.
The young woman walks up and down on the beach talking. Her hair is dark and cut short, her eyes are green. She walks there in 1911, 1926, 1985. No one will drive Marina away from there. The woman, Russian, always rests her head on her arms again. Her dead lips are not dead. And her dress flutters in the wind.

The sound of worn-out dresses, former steps. And somewhere still the rain of those times. Someone closes the window. Dora. Marina. Why do I cling tightly to the two of you, with so many lives around me? On the tables lie exercise books full of poems, someone is taking off his shoes. In the dark, nameless space two girls are laughing. Neither sorrow nor a false life can reach there.

There is a current of words which are written in foreign lands. Then as today. People like what is unknown.

The child sits in a house of memories and looks at the paper. The child sits and grows, and its sketches fade. They are put away in drawers, thrown into the trash. What makes some of them eternal is what a person saves while he lives, exists.

Marina is preserved in what is written. There are no comparisons.
That is life.

The actress Dora knits a scarf in a white room in Zagreb. She has probably forgotten everything. At night, perhaps, Marina sits beside her, smoking.